POLITE ENEMIES
(Buffalo Series Book 1)

by

JoAnn Smith Ainsworth

WHISKEY CREEK PRESS
www.whiskeycreekpress.com

Published by
WHISKEY CREEK PRESS
Whiskey Creek Press
PO Box 51052
Casper, WY 82605-1052
www.whiskeycreekpress.com

ISBN: 978-1-61160-590-7

Cover Artist: Angela Archer
Editor: Dave Field
Printed in the United States of America

Dedication

Dedicated to my nephews and niece—Bob, Ron, John, Jim, Philip and Heather.

My thanks to my critique partners and my friends who read early versions of the manuscript. Special thanks to Dr. Euleta Johnson.

Disclaimer: Although the town of Buffalo is real, all persons are fictitious, except some historical personages.

Chapter 1

Buffalo, Wyoming, 1895

Ida Louise Osterbach glanced up from slopping the hogs to see two rough looking men on the dirt lane leading to her farmhouse. They rode at a steady clip in the crisp spring air—like men with a purpose.

The way they sat their saddles was unfamiliar. Although Wyoming was much safer than when she and her late husband arrived almost ten years earlier, these were still precarious times. The Johnson County range war had only recently ended. The tiny hairs on the back of Ida's neck rose. She'd better not get caught out in the open. The men were planting the north acres so she and her friend, Peggy Knapp, were alone.

Ida dropped the empty bucket and hurried across the packed-earth barnyard toward the open kitchen door. She rubbed sweat off her forehead with the back of her sleeve as she ran. When close to the open kitchen doorway, she yelled out to alert Peggy.

"Strangers coming!"

As she rushed into the warmed kitchen, Ida peeled off dirty work gloves and wiped sweaty hands down the sides of the coarse pants she wore when working outside of the house.

The usually cheerful Peggy was frowning as she vigorously pumped water into a metal washbasin in the kitchen sink. "We don't often get riders we don't know around here." She splashed water over the flour dust coating her plump hands and arms up to her elbows from baking bread. "Drifters looking for work, do you think?"

Ida secured the kitchen door by its heavy wooden bar.

"Not likely. They ride like they know where they're going and mean business when they get here. We'd best stay locked up until we know who they are."

Ida removed the broad-brimmed hat she wore to protect her skin from the sun. A strand of dark brown hair fell alongside her face when the hat snagged a hair pin, pulling it loose from the German-housefrau-like braid she wrapped around her head. She brushed her hand at it, but didn't take the time to reset the pin before grabbing two pistols and a tin box of ammunition from the cabinet in the kitchen sideboard.

"Whatever could they want, I wonder?" Peggy briskly wiped spilled flour and lard off the table. She threw the damp burlap rag over the faucet of the kitchen pump before sliding bullets into the chambers of the pistols Ida placed on the newly cleaned oilcloth covering. "We're too far off the main road for them to think they're headed for town."

"Let's go see." Ida slid the last cartridge into the chamber of her pistol. Gripping a gun with her left hand, she hurried from the kitchen into the narrow hallway leading to the front of the house. The grandfather clock in the seldom-used parlor struck the half-hour as she sped by. She cautiously opened the porthole in the upper half of the front door to peer out at the two armed men. Both appeared to be in their forties. They had reined up some distance from her front porch. Controlling their impatient horses, they waited for her to acknowledge them.

"At least they follow visitor etiquette," she muttered—relieved, but still cautious.

The man taking the lead had curly blond hair showing from underneath a wide-brimmed hat shading startlingly blue eyes from the morning sun. For some reason, his attitude got Ida's back up. His ruggedly handsome face looked self-assured despite displaying signs of dissipation. A flamboyantly colorful kerchief tied around his neck created a striking contrast to skin weathered by long hours outdoors. The six-shooters on both hips were tied-down.

The other man's fierce scowl and hardened eyes were not hidden by his oversized, black sombrero. An unkempt, handle-bar mustache sagged. This gloomy man sat his horse with such malevolent stillness that Ida's skin crawled as when a scorpion brushes past. She fingered the extra cartridges she'd slipped into her deep pants pocket.

Peggy arrived, puffing from exertion and carrying a pistol. She leaned against the storage seat of the mirrored coat rack before nodding toward the open porthole. "Know them?"

Ida gave way at the door, shaking her head. "You?"

Her considerably shorter friend rose on tiptoes.

"No one I know," Peggy said after her turn at the opening.

"Guess we'd better find out who they are. Stand back."

Ida's heart stepped up a beat as she opened the upper half of the Dutch door. "Who are you? What do you want?" She cocked the pistol.

"No need for that, Ma'am." The blond-haired man gestured toward the gun. He spoke in a shadily cultured Southern voice and edged his horse closer. "We're here to be sociable."

His cohort stayed in place and didn't look the least bit sociable.

"Who are you?"

"Beau Campbell, Ma'am." He touched the brim of his hat. "Nephew to your estimable neighbor."

A shiver of repugnance traveled the length of Ida's spine on hearing the Campbell name. "Get off my property. You're not welcome here."

"Now, now, Miz Osterbach, let's not start our acquaintanceship on the wrong foot."

His smooth-tongued manner reminded Ida of the snake-oil salesman who worked Buffalo last summer. Her throat felt like her voice would get stuck, but she managed to spit out, "Being a relative of Rattlesnake is no recommendation. Get off my land."

"*¡Puta*," the cohort muttered. Although under his breath, Ida heard and her back stiffened.

The smooth-tongued man brazenly stayed where he was, doffed his hat and smiled ingratiatingly. "I'm here to make a magnificent offer for the purchase of your farm."

He kept misusing the English language while trying to sound high class. She stepped away from the Dutch door. "I'm not interested."

"Hold on there, Ma'am. Hear me out."

Ida stepped forward again. "You've got two minutes."

"Uncle Art's retiring, Ma'am, and I'm taking over his ranch. Your farm and his ranch will make a good-sized spread with plenty of water." He put his hat back on his head. "I'd make it worth your estimable while to sit down for a talk. I'll pay in gold—more than fair price."

He smiled a broad smile that some women might find captivating, but Ida didn't. She was glad her nemesis neighbor was giving up ranching, but his nephew looked to be as bad.

"I'm not selling." She started closing the wooden half panel.

"Wait." Beau dismounted his stallion and strode toward her. "Running a farm's too hard for a lady."

"Not for this woman," she said emphatically. "And stay right there. Any closer and I'll shoot."

Beau stopped, raising his hands in a mocking gesture of surrender. "Living out here's not safe. Ladies should live in town."

She raised the pistol and placed a shot into the ground close enough to raise dust and startle his horse so it twisted around, almost pulling the reins out of his hand.

"I can take care of myself."

"I can see that, Ma'am."

"Even if I was interested in selling, I'd never sell to a

Campbell. Your uncle murdered my husband."

Anger contorted Beau's face, but he took a deep breath and seemed to gain control so he could speak in the rational tones of a successful salesman. "My innocent uncle was cleared of that charge, Ma'am. Your husband and Uncle Art were getting ready for a fist fight, putting their holsters to one side, when the gun accidentally went off."

"Right through my husband's back and into his heart." Her voice cracked with dredged-up emotion. "Some accident!"

"There were witnesses."

She burned hot with anger. "Your uncle's ranch hands. Paid thugs."

Beau's face darkened with the flush of blood from his anger. He clenched his fists.

"You're mistaken, Ma'am. I'll send Uncle Art over. He'll explain what happened."

Ida aimed the gun straight at Beau. "Rattlesnake knows better than to show his face around here. I'll put a bullet between his eyes if he tries."

"Let's go," the gloomy partner grumbled. "You're not getting anywhere."

"Good advice," Peggy yelled.

"Good riddance," Ida said.

With a roar, Beau dropped the reins and charged.

Taken aback by the fierceness released when he stripped away the thin layer of Southern charm, Ida's shoulder blades tightened and the back of her head started to pound. She swiftly lowered the gun to his groin. "One more step and I'll make a eunuch of you."

Beau stopped dead. He stared at her and must not have liked what he saw in either Ida or in Peggy, whose pistol was centered on his friend. He spun angrily on his heel, leaving indentations in the dust of the roadway as he stomped back to his horse.

"You'll regret this," he hissed as he mounted. "People didn't call my uncle 'Rattlesnake' for nothing and I'm worse."

Whirling his horse around, he galloped down the road.

Beau's evil-eyed cohort sat a moment, scowling, then slowly turned his horse to follow.

A shiver traveled down Ida's spine.

* * * *

Minutes later, Peggy placed a steaming pewter mug of sugared tea on the oil cloth-covered kitchen table where Ida sat, hunched over and weary. The confrontation with Campbell had taken a toll. She wrapped trembling fingers around the warmed mug and sipped. The tea's soothing herbal aroma started working its calming effects.

Ida blessed the day she decided to give Peggy a home after her husband's early death to disease. Peggy ran the farmhouse efficiently and cooked superb meals. This released Ida—in good conscience—to work the fields.

"The nerve of him." Peggy looked thoroughly upset. "Wouldn't you think a Campbell would be ashamed to show his face around here?"

Ida willed her heartbeat to slow down. "They're still trying to get their hands on my water." She pictured the series of irrigation ditches in the sloping fields that fed water from Clear Creek to her crops. The creek continued on, running through Campbell property to water a straggly herd of cattle. "Art Campbell says I siphon off too much."

"Horsefeathers!" Peggy passed by on her way to the cook stove. "Art settled here after you and Dean. He knew what he was getting into."

"That man lacks common sense. He overgrazed for the amount of water on his land."

"He's okay in good years," Peggy said, "but in dry years he's not."

"He should've dug wells, but he never figured it out until his cattle started dying. Still hasn't done it. Just keeps hassling me." Ida sipped the sweetened tea. "He killed Dean for our water."

"By keeping the farm going," Peggy said, "you cooked Art's goose."

Ida remembered how—newly widowed—she'd assumed control of the hundred and sixty acres in the foothills of the Big Horn Mountains near the Bozeman Trail to Buffalo. It had been a struggle, but with the help of her cousin, Ernest, she'd made it. "But his nephew's trying to horn in and whitewash the shooting."

"Remember, sweetie, the sheriff said there wasn't enough evidence. He said it must've been accidental, didn't he?"

Ida grimaced. "They'll never convince me."

Peggy puckered her brow. "Should we ask Mr. Buell for help, do you think? Remember, honey, he wanted to buy the farm after Dean got shot. He won't like to hear that someone else is muscling in, will he?"

Ida's face flushed. She and her rancher neighbor on the

south side hadn't spoken in two years. "I'm not about to ask that beanpole for help. He hasn't been civil since we quarreled."

"It was just a thought." Peggy made herself a mug of tea, stirred in sugar and milk and placed it on the table.

"I can take care of myself. I don't need that man to fight my battles."

"I know that, sweetie."

"Besides, Mr. high and mighty Jared Buell has never been partial to farmers planted next to his precious ranch." Ida still warmed her hands on the mug.

Peggy said, wistfully, "You'll never be more than polite enemies, will you?"

"He's lucky I'm even that cordial." And to think, her friend, Martha, once suggested she set her cap for the wealthy widower.

Peggy lifted a ladle and tasted the stew heating on the wood-burning cook stove. "Food's ready. I'd best get the men in from the fields."

She unbarred the kitchen door and gave three resounding clangs on the dinner bell mounted just outside to summon Ernest and the two field hands.

Ida drank the last of her tea before getting up to help Peggy set the table. "They'll be getting bad news with their meal."

* * * *

A half hour later, Beau Campbell sprawled onto a dilapidated kitchen chair in his Uncle Art's ranch house and poured himself a shot of rot-gut whiskey from the bottle on the table. The tin cup was anything but clean, but Beau didn't care. He'd drunk out of worse.

Anger as hot as a blacksmith's fire coursed through his veins. He'd just told his uncle, a man in his late fifties, his back bowed from pain, about the debacle at the farm.

"Telled ya so," his uncle said.

"Damn that infernal woman. She'll regret it."

"Watch yer step," Art warned. He gulped a slug of whiskey straight from the bottle. "She stirred up a hornet's nest when I kilt her Dean."

"I need her water to make this ranch pay off."

"Tried gettin' that water myself. Didn't work out. You'll need some smarts to git on 'er good side."

"Trust me, Old Man, I've got the smarts. I would've been languishing in jail long before this if I didn't."

His uncle owned land near the abandoned Fort Reno, but had been too lazy or too ignorant to work the size herd needed to make it productive. It was suspected by the town folk that some of the butchered meat he managed to sell to the railroad at Clearmont was from cattle rustled from neighboring towns in Sheridan County. Beau knew that to be so.

Six months ago, Art badly injured his back in a street brawl. His uncle could no longer prevent hired hands from taking more than their due. Beau had received Art's letter at his Missouri house offering the ranch in exchange for board and protection. He'd honor that obligation—unless it was no longer convenient.

Lucky for him that letter arrived when it did. A few days before, irate husbands had almost run Beau out of a town on a rail. These prominent citizens had told him in no uncertain terms to leave and not come back. He'd sold his property at favorable terms to the men who wanted to see the back of him and was wondering what to do next when his uncle's letter had arrived. The offer gave him a second chance to build a respectable façade and enjoy his stash of money from train and bank robberies.

Dammit. He needed that blasted farm to get close to an old enemy of his. He'd use the land to launch raids to torment and destroy his resilient adversary.

"I'll get her out of there." Beau gritted his teeth.

Art spit tobacco juice. "Don't yer count on it. That bitch is tough."

Chapter 2

Jared Buell rode his powerful gelding along a dirt road bordered by distant, snow-capped mountain peaks toward his two-thousand-acre Bar J ranch. At almost forty-two, he could look back with pride to what he'd accomplished. He'd carved a profitable ranch out of Wyoming wilderness, defending it against renegade Indians looking for his scalp, and Texan range-war invaders.

He and his foreman, Russell Quentin, were returning from transacting business in Buffalo. Both wore town clothes and he thought his burly foreman looked uncomfortable in the starched, white cotton, band collar. Truth be told, Jared himself could hardly wait to shuck these clothes. He felt at his best in riding gear.

"Rattlesnake's nephew tried to sweet talk the Osterbach widow out of her farm," Russ said. "Got chased away with a gun."

"Except that it's a Campbell doing the buying, I'd be glad to see that female bulldog gone from there. No decent woman should be working in the fields." Irritation settled between Jared's shoulder blades.

Russ—a no-nonsense, muscular man in his early thirties—looked at him. "She probably thought you were trying
to drive her off. You still pissed off?"

"Of course not." Jared drew himself taller with a big intake of air. "My offer to buy her farm after Dean was killed
was an act of charity." He sounded supercilious even to
himself.

An amused expression crossed Russ' face. "You trying
to convince me the offer had nothing to do with her being a
good-looking woman? Don't try to bamboozle me, old
friend."

Jared felt himself flush. Even though it was six years
since his wife passed, he didn't think of women that way.
Isabella was the love of his life. No other woman could fill
her shoes. "Of course not," he said again. "I knew she'd be
strapped for cash for the funeral. Besides, I assumed she'd
be sensible like most women and go back east to her family."

"Instead, she convinced her cousin to join her and kept
the farm going," Russ said. "Put a burr under your saddle,
did it?"

Before Jared could think of a reply, he heard a rider
coming fast toward them. He touched the butt of his gun and
unhooked its leather safety strap. His irritation grew when
the man didn't slow down, but galloped past, his black Stetson almost completely blocking his face and his horse kicking up considerable dust from its pounding hooves.

Jared reined in and turned to stare down the road at the
man's receding back. A glimmer of recognition brought a
scowl. A vise tightened on his heart even as he shook his

head in denial. It couldn't be. Not in his own back yard.

"Know him?" Russ asked after the rider dropped out of sight.

"I may."

For years, he'd been chasing, without success, a man who'd killed his brother and sister-in-law during a bank robbery. The Kansas posse had decimated the murdering gang—except for its cunning leader. He'd slipped away—saving his life, but leaving behind the bank's gold.

Jared had left the ranch in Russ' hands for long periods of time while he hunted. He'd been gone when Isabella sickened and died. Jared knew that the guilt of his not being there for his beloved wife colored his current perspective of women. "His build reminds me of the man I've been chasing the past nine years—the one who murdered my brother and his pregnant wife."

His foreman sounded anxious. "That was Rattlesnake's nephew."

Jared was taken by surprise. "Son of a bitch."

"He just moved to Wyoming. I met him last week in the saloon."

Jared's brain dredged up details from almost a decade ago. Same build. Same hair color. The bank robber wasn't named Campbell, but names could be changed. Had the fugitive he'd been chasing for almost a decade taken up residence in his own back yard? He couldn't be sure.

Russ interrupted his thoughts. "Some say Art was an outlaw before he took up ranching. Could be his nephew is one."

Jared gritted his teeth. "If I'm right, that Osterbach

woman's up against a man without a moral bone in his body."

* * * *

Beau Campbell's spine still felt the chill of unexpectedly riding headlong toward the man who'd haunted him all these years. At the last minute, he'd recognized Buell because of the Bar J foreman. He was able to cover his face with his Stetson, gallop past and resist the temptation to look back.

"Dammit to hell," he muttered.

Since arriving in Buffalo, he'd made a point of staying out of his adversary's way. He needed time to build up a gang. It wouldn't be to full strength for months. Its members were slowly arriving a few at a time. Beau wanted the town's citizens to get used to seeing small groups of his riders around town and to take them in stride. No reason to alarm the good folk before he was ready—ready to eliminate Jared Buell.

He'd come up against Buell in Kansas. He'd robbed a bank and killed the bank owner and his wife. The posse following him was relentless, the damage from bullets significant. One after another, members of his gang and of the posse were killed or injured badly enough to be out of the game. Finally, the fight was down to him, the sheriff and Buell. He'd managed to gut-shoot the sheriff, which kept Buell busy while he got away. If it weren't that he'd always had a way with women, he would've been caught and hung.

Wounded, his gang decimated, the bank gold retaken by the posse, he'd slunk penniless into the hills. He stumbled across the lonely mountain cabin of a widowed woman and had hit the jackpot. She'd nursed him and fed him for favors easily rendered. By the time he'd left—when her wrangler cousin returned from a trail ride—he was back to health with a new plan in mind. He'd spent years re-building his gang and had gotten rich once again from train and bank robberies. Tired of rough riding, he now craved a more peaceful life. The one he'd built for himself in Missouri was destroyed because of his philandering. He'd not make that mistake here.

Beau reined in his horse and turned to ride cross country to Art's place—his place once all the legal papers of transfer were prepared and signed. The jaunt to town was meant to set up his solid-citizen persona. It would have to wait. This brush with the rancher forced a change. If Buell had recognized him, he'd be showing up at Art's—possibly with guns blazing. Beau needed to be ready.

Hatred for the rancher seared his heart. He'd nearly died from their last encounter. This time, he intended to stack the deck in his favor.

* * * *

Jared wasn't content to wait and wonder if the rider was the murderer he'd sought for nearly a decade. He decided to return to town and confront him.

After ordering Russ to continue on to the Bar J to let his daughter know he'd be late coming home tonight, he turned his horse toward Buffalo. There he prowled the dusty streets and noisy public places, but—just like that will-o'-the-wisp Kansas outlaw—this man was nowhere in sight.

Frustration built with each failure.

These days, he was operating from a dim memory of the

fleeting glimpses he'd gotten as the man sneaked through the forest to evade the posse. For the longest time, Jared had carried a hand-drawn wanted poster of the man. Eventually it had deteriorated into unusable pieces. Even the memory began to fade as no hint of the gang leader's whereabouts surfaced in the outlaw rumor mills.

Jared had searched frantically for this man, in part to cancel out the guilt he felt for not being closer to his brother those last years in Kansas. It was one of those things where the wives didn't get along. It was easier to keep a distance rather than create conflict at home.

Jared leaned against a store porch post to think.

Was this or wasn't this the outlaw who had murdered his brother? Earlier today, he thought he'd recognized the rider's build. Now, he was beginning to doubt his senses.

He pushed away from the wooden post and walked hurriedly along Main Street toward the telegraph office. Before instigating a confrontation, he'd better be sure he had the right man. He needed to hire a Pinkerton detective.

Removing his Stetson, he stepped through the narrow doorway of the recently opened telegraph office. Before this establishment set up a shop on Main Street, he'd had to ride to the fort to send a message.

He walked toward a scarred, wooden counter where an older man wearing an eye shade was rolling up white shirt sleeves to expose thin forearms.

"Good afternoon, Mr. McGregor."

"Afternoon, Mr. Buell. What can I do for you today?"

"I need to send a telegram, but, first, I'm looking for information." The telegraph office was a central place of gossip and he often took advantage of that hub of knowledge. "There's a new man in town. I wondered what you'd heard about him."

"Which one? There's always a new man riding into this town."

"Art Campbell's nephew."

"Oh, him." The telegraph operator shrugged as if to confess he didn't know much. "He's been in a few times. Nice enough fella."

"No bad talk about him?"

"Not that I've heard. He's sociable. The ladies love him."

Jared's interest was picking up. The Kansas outlaw was a favorite with the ladies. Campbell could be his man.

"Hails from Missouri," McGregor added. "He had property there."

The brief flare of excitement drained out. "You sure?"

"He's been sending telegrams to exchange money from a Missouri bank to your bank. You must have seen him over there."

Jared shook his head. "Not so far."

"Really? You're in and out the bank all the time. What with board meetings and ranch business, I felt sure you must've met him."

Jared was confused. He knew of no tie ins of the Kansas gang to another state.

"Sold his Missouri property so he could re-settle here and help out his uncle." The telegraph operator tidied the counter, aligning stacks of reports and forms. "He has the law office drawing up papers to take over the ranch."

Tension drained out of Jared. Campbell wasn't his man. He wasn't a man constantly riding the outlaw trail, but someone who owned property. A mistake—and yet the impression made as he galloped by was so strong.

"You think he's here to stay—not just passing through?"

"From what I've seen," McGregor said, "he's here to stay. Even put his name down for membership in one of the social clubs. Why do you ask?"

Jared didn't want to say. He wouldn't malign an innocent man. "It's not important. I'll just send that telegram."

McGregor pushed a yellow form across the counter. "Fill this out. Remember, you pay by the word."

Jared carried the yellow paper to the sturdy, but scarred writing desk set against a side wall. The furniture had been transferred in from the fort's telegraph office when it shut down. He picked up an ink pen from the grooved slot at the top of the desk and used the tip of his index finger to test that the metal point was sharp. Damaged nubs tore the paper or caused ink blots. Satisfied, he slid the point into its wooden handle, unscrewed the cap of the stained inkpot, and dipped the pen point.

He printed out the Pinkerton message, asking the agency to assign the investigator he'd used in the past. He wanted to determine if the warrant for his brother's murderer was still active and, if so, to get another wanted poster. The difficulty for their investigation was that the murders were nine years ago and the witnesses were all back in Kansas—if still alive. He left out any reference linking Campbell to the murders, but did ask for a report on Beau's life style and sale of property in Missouri. He'd warn McGregor to keep this telegram to himself.

It took a lot of words and was expensive, but the peace of mind would be well worth it.

Chapter 3

"Fire in the west pasture," Todd Mason yelled to Ida and Ernest early Friday morning as he frantically rode toward them where they were planting potatoes. Todd, a teenager who often helped with the harvest, lived on the neighboring Bar J where his mother worked as the ranch cook. He reined in his horse as he shouted, "Great Godfrey, Miz Osterbach, I was riding by and seen the hay shack afire."

Ida's gut twisted with fear. That was the land she kept in native grass as winter fodder for the animals. She and Ernest dropped the potatoes, grabbed their hoes and the empty potato sacks, and ran toward the west pasture. Todd turned his horse and rode ahead of them. When he got over the crest, he pointed and said, "There."

She could see the smoke now. Panic built. She felt a tightness in her chest and her breath seemed more labored. She never underestimated the swift deviousness of a prairie fire.

"Ride to the farmhouse," Ida yelled to Todd as she ran. "Get Peggy to bring those old rugs we use to beat out fires.

Get Buck and Hank to stop the fence mending at the corral to help us."

She thought briefly about it and then made up her mind.

"Better alert the Bar J, too. The fire could spread onto Buell's land."

* * * *

Ida arrived in the west pasture out of breath, but determined not to be bested. She vigorously hoed dirt onto the grass fire as Ernest tackled the flames in the shack. With a couple of potato sacks swung in each hand, he slapped resoundingly time and again at the edges of the fire to smother it. Two sides of the shack were already burned out. The escaping smoke was thick, black and acrid from the tarpaper weatherproofing. Fortunately, the pungent smoke spiraled straight up. No wind.

Looking through the burned-out side, Ida saw that the fire hadn't started naturally. A pile of greasy rags was the culprit. Yet, there hadn't ever been rags in this shack—greasy or otherwise. Anger rose. Somebody had deliberately started the fire. Outrage fueled her, making her more determined to beat back and smother the fire.

Peggy arrived driving the wagon with the farm hands, Buck and Hank, on the seat. It was stacked with old rugs, leather throws, tools and four buckets of water to wet down the rugs. The field hands jumped off and unloaded so Peggy could maneuver the wagon and Old Molly a safe distance from the fire. Ernest abandoned the shack as a lost cause and joined the others in tackling the grass fires.

All of them were hard at work when the Bar J men—Jared, Russ, Todd and two wranglers—rode up. Fear showed in the whites of their horses' eyes from smelling smoke. Their mounts slid to a stop and trotted quickly away after the men jumped off.

Ida was struck dumb. She never expected her unfriendly neighbor to step onto her farm land. She thought he'd wait until the fire reached his ranch. That he didn't wait caused a dichotomy of emotions. One was relief that there were four extra pairs of hands to fight the fire. The opposite was consternation that she would be beholden to Jared Buell.

"Rugs and tools are over there," Peggy shouted to the new arrivals. "Glad to have the help."

Wasting no time, the men rushed to grab a tool or a rug and spread out to augment the efforts already underway. The skin at the back of Ida's neck tightened when the rancher trotted in her direction and hoed the ground to her left and slightly forward. The last time they were this close they were shouting at one another. He was calling her "pigheaded" and she was calling him "underhanded."

Relieved that Peggy broke the ice, Ida took this opportunity to re-collect her thoughts until she could eventually say, "Good of you to come," with some semblance of servility.

"Never hurts to have extra hands in this kind of circumstance," he said.

Slightly out of breath from rising smoke which made it hard to breathe, she assured him, "We'll get the fire out…it won't spread."

Not being a farmer, Jared didn't know how to properly hold the hoe he plied so awkwardly, but the vigor he put behind each downward stroke overcame that deficiency. "How did it start?"

"Deliberately set." She was breathing heavily from exertion.

"Really?"

"Greasy rags. We don't keep rags…in fodder sheds."

Jared's eyebrows raised. "Do you know who?"

"Nothing…I can prove…I have suspicions." She'd never had this kind of trouble until Campbell showed up wanting to buy her out.

She took a moment to brush back the dark brown hair escaping her braid. She probably got smudges of soot on her flushed cheek and perspiring temples.

Oh, well, she thought, *it isn't as if I have to make a good impression.*

She decided to start a fire break past the outer rim of the fire, hoping that a wide-enough dirt patch would stop the flames there. She grabbed her hoe in her left hand, a pitch fork in the right, and took the opportunity during the short walk to catch her breath. To her surprise, Jared followed her.

"I see what you're doing," he said. "Good idea."

She didn't need praise from Jared Buell to know she was doing the right thing.

Attacking the earth in front of her, he broke through the network of roots. She came along behind to turn the earth and bury the weeds and grass to deprive the fire of fuel. It was early enough in the season that there was plenty of moisture in the vegetation and the soil. If arson was tried during the months when the grasses had dried, she might not have had a chance to contain a fire. She cast an eye on the others and saw they were making strong progress.

Jared worked with his shirt off, his back muscles rippling under the morning sun. She marveled at his strength. The skinny beanpole of a rancher who spent his days on a horse was definitely not a weakling.

While she'd been focused on his muscles, he'd gotten well ahead of her. With increased vigor, Ida narrowed the gap. There was no way she'd let him show her up on her own farm.

Twenty minutes later, the fire was down to smoldering embers and her fire break hadn't been needed. The shack was a total loss. Fortunately, all the hay stored in it last year had been consumed during the winter months. The animals now had new-growth meadow grass to eat. It would be at least three months before she'd need to rebuild.

The acrid smell from the charred earth seeped into her consciousness, causing anger to rise from the base of her spine. She was sure Beau Campbell was to blame for this, but there was no way to prove it. She calmed her anger and turned to her rancher neighbors.

"Thanks for lending a hand," Ida said to the Bar J men as she stripped off her gloves and threw them into the bed of the wagon into which Hank was stacking the farming tools. "Come with us to the farmhouse for a piece of Peggy's pies."

It was the least she could do for the extra pairs of hands.

Immediately, Russ grinned broadly and Ida suspected the Bar J ranch foreman had as much interest in Peggy as he did in her pie. If relations thawed between the ranch owner and herself, maybe she could suggest to her friend that she should take an interest in the reliable, hardworking foreman.

Ernest volunteered to stay behind to watch for hot spots.

"Here," Buck said, tossing a rifle to her cousin, who caught it with ease. "Use my gun to signal if you need us back here."

"You bet."

Ida tried to peel her sweaty shirt away from her sticky body so that it could dry a little as she walked. She guessed she smelled as badly as Jared, who reeked of sweat and smoke.

* * * *

Jared had thought twice about accepting the invitation to the farmhouse. In the end, he decided he'd better accept. Campbell was trying to make himself Jared's neighbor by buying the farm. If there was any buying to be done, he wanted Ida Osterbach to look to him, not Campbell. He needed to set up some rapport with this farmer. Allies against a common enemy would suffice.

Her masculine clothing emphasized her muscular frame but—having watched her turn the earth—he knew there was no flab underneath. The rough work shirt she wore clung damply to a generous bosom. There was a nice roll to the hips when she walked. When she bent over, her breeches pulled tightly against a womanly swell of buttocks. He may not approve of her way of life, but he could appreciate the muscles it put on a woman and the well-built female the heavy work had produced.

This brought up a second reason for staying for pie—he found her attractive. It had been years since he'd had a response to a woman. That the attraction happened while fighting a fire and not while at a church social dumbfounded him.

Leading his stallion—which had returned when he'd whistled—he hurried to walk alongside her as she headed toward the farmhouse. A slight frown crossed her face when he approached, as if she was annoyed that he'd caught up with her. *Too bad, my dear,* he thought, *I have my own agenda to follow.*

She's almost as tall as I am, he thought—markedly different from his petite Isabella, who had to take two steps for every one of his.

Jared couldn't imagine his blond wife having a hair out of place—or even looking as if it were about to happen. Ida's hair threatened to profusely burst from its practical braid. He pictured that dark, thick hair cascading to a naked waistline. A few buttons undone near that impressive bosom wouldn't hurt either.

Jared's shoulders and back ached. Already his hands had grown painful blisters.

Give me twelve hours in a saddle, he thought, *to a half day bending over a hoe. How does she do it?*

His reaction today differed radically from formerly. True he'd thought Ida striking the few times he'd seen her over the years, but that was as far as his interest went. At Dean's funeral, her face was drawn and careworn. She'd still looked haggard when they fell out over the sale of her property. Since then, they'd kept a frigid distance. Today had changed all that.

"It was most kind of you, Mr. Buell," he heard her say somewhat formally, "to come so quickly. We haven't been on the best of terms. You may have been reluctant to get involved."

"Just being neighborly," he heard himself say, not speaking the whole truth by hiding the fact that he wanted to insert himself between Campbell and a possible sale of the farm. If her property was destroyed, she might take Campbell gold rather than rebuild. Jared wanted to ward that off.

"Still, it was good of you."

Truth be told, he'd expected a larger blaze. From the way Todd Mason had described the fire, he thought his ranch was about to be threatened by an inferno.

"I hear you're being pressured to sell by Art Campbell's nephew," he said.

She nodded. "He talked sweet to me when he came to my door, but he had two guns strapped on and tied down. And his companion was scary."

"Be extra careful, Ma'am. Campbell could be an outlaw."

A frown quickly marred Ida's forehead. "I thought he might be behind the arson, trying to burn me out since I wouldn't sell when he asked."

"If he's the man I think he is, I wouldn't put it past him."

"There's no way to prove it."

"You should inform the sheriff's office," Jared said. "Even without proof, it's best that they know."

"I will…next time someone's in town."

They walked in silence for a while, then he asked, "Did you make some of the pies?" He could think of no other way to re-open the conversation. He longed for the social dexterity of his late wife.

"I don't bake anymore."

"She was great with crusts in her day." Peggy spoke from the seat of the wagon as she guided Old Molly over uneven ground and headed for the barn. "And she would win cake baking contests. Isn't that true, Ida?"

"Those days are gone. I need all my strength for the fields. I've no time for the kitchen."

Jared scowled. Just the opposite of what a lady should be doing. His late wife would never have neglected her womanly duties by taking on a man's job.

* * * *

Ida ushered everyone inside the large farm kitchen. Sunlight poured through the un-shuttered windows, creating dancing patterns on the linoleum floor from free-floating dust motes. When she and Dean first built, the kitchen was their only room. Everything about their life together in those early days originated from this room. In the slow times of winter, it was still her favorite as they talked or read aloud while the heat from the iron cook stove kept everyone toasty.

As the men passed through the doorway, she wondered if Jared would find her home up to his high standards. Maybe her parlor would pass muster, but today wasn't a parlor occasion.

I am who I am, she thought. *This is the best I can do.*

Before being seated, each man washed up at the kitchen sink in a blue-enameled basin filled with lye soap suds and freshly pumped water. Todd brought towels from the pantry before climbing stairs two at a time to bring down chairs from the two bedrooms where she and Peggy slept. Ernest slept in the bunkhouse with the hired hands.

With a shuffling of feet across the hardwood floor, each man claimed an empty chair around the long table as Ida set out plates, mugs, forks and spoons. She debated on getting the cloth napkins out of the sideboard cupboard, but decided against it. A sooty smell clung to everyone's clothing. No sense creating a laundry problem by transferring that smell to the good linen.

Peggy arrived slightly out of breath, having stabled Old Molly in the barn.

The joking and scraping of chairs as the men jostled for seats hauntingly reminded Ida that the depth of her heart-wrenching sorrow blighted other aspects of her life. Entertaining had halted at the farmhouse after her husband's death. Today, dynamic male energy and laughter bounced off the walls of her cozy kitchen, creating nostalgia.

Maybe this year I'll plan a harvest hoe-down, she thought.

Peggy lifted the big, blue-enameled coffeepot from where it sat throughout the day on the low heat at the back of the wood-burning stove to place it on a metal trivet in the center of the table. Ida cut slices of berry and rhubarb pies which Peggy had created from last year's canned fruit. Todd got the cream and sugar from the pantry.

Ida said to Todd, "When you finish eating, take some pie and coffee out to Ernest. He must be feeling neglected by now."

"Will do, Miz Osterbach," he said as he claimed a large slice of rhubarb pie. He dug in with gusto.

She and Peggy kept the coffee mugs filled and urged slices of pie on the men as they hashed and re-hashed fighting the fire. Eventually all pies were consumed and the last of the coffee drunk. Her anger had calmed. After all, some tramp could've slept in the hay shed and left the rags behind. She shouldn't unfairly condemn the nephew because she despised the uncle.

The men leaned back in their chairs, cleaning their teeth with wooden toothpicks.

Ida kept a cut crystal toothpick holder on the table whether for everyday meals or for special occasions. A wedding present from her Illinois family, this cut crystal was a quality that even someone as rich as Jared could admire. He lifted it and looked carefully at the heavy, sharp-edged crystal before he took a toothpick—as if he had heard her thoughts.

As everyone was saying farewell, Ida handed Todd a metal box to deliver to Ernest with a large slice of pie in it and a tin container filled with coffee laced with heavy cream.

"Todd, you can take some of those buttermilk biscuits you like that are stored in the tin on the sideboard. You deserve a treat for spotting the fire."

He eagerly lifted off the tin lid and stuffed four biscuits into his pockets.

"Thanks, Ma'am."

Exhausted, Ida waited impatiently as her farm hands filed out to the bunkhouse. She and Peggy needed to finish cleaning the kitchen so they could start supper. Then it was milking the cows and feeding the chickens and mucking out the horse stall.

She was weary to the bone, but it would be a while before she could finally get to bed to rest. Dawn with its chores came early.

* * * *

Jared, exhausted, his clothes reeking from smoke and stiff with grime, slowly rode homeward with his foreman at his side. His wranglers had long ago ridden off to check on the cattle for the night. He eyed the darkening snow-covered Big Horn peaks as he guided his horse toward the kerosene-lit ranch house. Images of his farmer neighbor swirled in his mind. "Mrs. Osterbach is better-looking than I remembered, not so gaunt as when her husband died." He hadn't intended to speak, but something compelled him to get her name out of his mouth and make her real.

"Dean's death hit her hard," Russ said. "She lost a lot of weight back then."

"Seems solidly packed now."

Russ chuckled.

"Manual labor does that."

Jared stayed quiet for a while before saying, "I never see her in town." Civic and bank duties made him spend a great deal of time in Buffalo. When her husband was alive, he used to see her in town from time to time. Now, he didn't see her. Ernest and Peggy, but not Ida.

"She doesn't much care for town," his foreman said. "She says she gets all the company she wants at the farm."

In many ways, Jared himself was a loner. Town folk didn't understand what it was like to willingly live in comfort with the loneliness of the land.

"She's really good at managing that farm, if you ask

me," Russ said. "She rotates her crops, keeps her books up-to-date and works like a horse."

Jared appreciated an owner who kept an eye on income and expenses. One quick way to lose a homestead was to overspend. At the bank, he'd rescued many a title-holder who'd gotten into trouble.

He swatted at a fly buzzing around his horse's head.

"I'm worried," he heard himself say. "If Beau is who I think he is, and if he could get away with it, I believe he'd slit her throat to get the farm."

"She won't give up easily," Russ said.

"I know. That's why I'm worried.

Chapter 4

Crack!

Ida instinctively dropped flat onto the freshly turned soil into which she and her cousin were planting potatoes. A second rifle bullet whizzed over her head, kicking up dirt near where she was hiding. Her heart raced and her breath came in fast bursts.

"Someone's shooting!"

Ernest Nolan—a golden-haired male version of the statuesque Ida—had been working several rows away. He'd already hit the ground, sheltered by the ridges of plowed earth. "Are you all right?"

"Fine."

Flattening her body into the pungent furrow, she raised her head just enough to see a man on horseback on distant Campbell land. It had been seven tense days since she'd last seen that huge sombrero. Before she could bring the figure into focus against the glare of the early morning sun, the man casually raised his rifle to the sky in a parody of a salute and shouted, "*Conejo.*"

"Rabbit, my ass," she muttered. Her pounding heart

echoed in her ears as she watched the rider slowly turn his horse and ride toward a man waiting farther back. Ida shivered at the deliberateness of it. "They can't get away with this."

She scrambled on all fours to the nearby wheelbarrow and a rifle leaning against it—the one they brought in case they spotted game. Steadying the gun against the edge of the wheelbarrow, she fired as close to the man and his horse as she could get—considering their increasing distance. The horse reacted with side steps, but the man in the sombrero ignored her shot. His self-control flooded her with unsettling emotions. She beat down the rising fear as she got up and dusted herself off.

"Damn," Ernest said as he rose to his feet. "Campbell's nephew wants you afraid to plant so you'll give up the farm."

"Never happen. I put too much into this farm to be run off."

Ida took a deep breath, allowing the aroma of tilled earth to fill her nostrils. "We'll all bring guns from now on." They hadn't needed guns in the fields since the range wars, but she'd make sure all hands could protect themselves.

"What about the rest of the day?" Ernest asked.

Ida bristled. He'd looked at her sympathetically. She didn't want pity.

"Finish planting," she said stubbornly, "just like we planned."

* * * *

A half hour later Beau Campbell, with Diablo Avilos at his side, entered his uncle's ranch kitchen. He grabbed up the whiskey bottle from the table and took a swallow before turning a kitchen chair backwards and straddling it.

"She'll skedaddle soon enough," Beau bragged to his mean-spirited uncle. "We're making it hard for her to work. She'll give up."

Art wagged a crooked index finger at his nephew. "Watch yerself. I don't want the sheriff snoopin' 'round."

"The *pinche* sheriff's out of town," Diablo informed Art.

Beau also assured his uncle, "I don't want the law here neither. Buell mustn't have recognized me the other day; otherwise, he'd have been out here. I don't want him getting interested because he hears a deputy was at the ranch."

Beau grimaced at Diablo. "You were supposed to create a hunting accident. Showing off with that shot was stupid."

"Wanted to see *la puta* jump."

Art spat tobacco juice into the tin in the corner. "Females. Always lettin' you down or gettin' in yer way." He gestured toward his nephew. "Bin that way since you wuz littl', isn't that the truth? Lost your ma when only twelve."

Beau still believed his mother chose to wither and die to be with her abusive soldier husband in a grave rather than stay alive to care for him. Her abandonment colored all his relationships with women. Her betrayal—layered onto his anger at the farmer woman—inflamed him. Blood pounded threateningly in his head. He hoped one of those blinding headaches wasn't coming on.

"That damn farmer woman…" He left his angry retort hanging in the air. The woman's refusal to sell stuck in his craw.

"Kill *la puta.* Be done with it," Diablo urged.

"Can't, my friend. I've reformed into the solid citizen my ma always wanted."

Art laughed sourly. "She giv' you all them highfalutin' manners. Where'd they getcha?"

His fallen society mother had taught him the manners and social graces that allowed him access to the better homes that thieves like him usually had no hope of entering, except to rob.

Beau preened. "The ladies love a southern gentleman."

"Crock a shit." His uncle spoke around a plug of tobacco. "I did all right with the ladies afore I hurt my back."

Diablo smirked. "Beau means respectable ladies."

"That's right, Uncle Art. I can't have people suspicious of me the way they are of you. I want to be invited into society circles."

"Can't prove I did no thievin'," his uncle said before spitting tobacco juice.

Beau knew that was true, but suspicion was perhaps worse. "Can't prove it, true, but you're never invited into the best houses."

"Don't want ta' be."

"Well, I do."

Chapter 5

That warm, spring evening, Ida wandered leisurely on the farmhouse road, the skirt of her lightly starched dress swishing softly. Ten years ago today, she and Dean had staked their claim to these acres. Exhaustion from onerous toil usually made her muscles ache each evening, but, tonight, she was in high spirits. Tonight, burdens were set aside. Tonight, she was just Ida. Not responsible landowner. Not faithful friend. Not reliable cousin. Just Ida.

The aroma of the cottonwoods filled the air and their discarded fluffy white balls covered the packed earth. A pistol weighed down one pocket in case Rattlesnake's nephew decided to visit. She'd have no trouble protecting herself from a rattlesnake—whether animal or human. She'd been taught to shoot by her friend, Annie Butler, who worked in the Sheridan Wild West Show as Annie Oakley.

To celebrate, she'd donned a flowered dress—putting aside the trousers and long-sleeved man's work shirt she usually wore to protect herself from brambles. The calf-high work boots which would safeguard her ankles from snake bite were cast aside for patent-leather slippers.

The fields behind the fences, the meadowlands stretching out in front of her, the farm buildings at her back—all prospered in her care. Her beloved Dean would've been proud.

Her good-sized farm had two cows, a few sheep—whose wool she exchanged with the seamstress in town for reduced-cost clothing—a horse, a couple of goats to eat the prairie grass close to the farm house, some pigs and several dozen chickens. Most of her land was in prairie grass which she cut from flood-irrigated pastures and dried for winter hay for the animals. A keen sense of fulfillment washed over her.

The sweat of their brows had flowed abundantly into this tilled earth and into a painstakingly built home. The farmhouse roof still held the sod laid during those first years. Short clumps of grass grew out of it each rainy season. Within a couple of years, they'd added the wide porch spanning the front of the house—her favorite place to relax after a hard day's work. Eventually, they could afford whitewash. She remembered Dean happily slapping bucketsful onto the weathered board. The farm buildings had grown to include a barn constructed with the help of friends, the bunkhouse where Ernest and the hired hands slept, and the storage sheds.

They'd planned their future on this land around an evening campfire. After setting up camp under a magnificent starlight sky, they'd made love with an intensity that outshone even those heavenly orbs. This was their place—a place to set down roots—the place to raise that family that never happened.

A cloud passed over the crescent moon. The enforced darkness matched the sadness gripping her heart. After suspicion became a certainty that she and Dean could never have children, they'd grown even closer—clinging solely to each other. A cricket chirped a solitary tune, a reminder that now she had to go it alone.

A pain as sharp as on the day she'd heard the news stabbed her heart. She stopped and drew in a deep breath. Burning anger rose from the base of her spine. The nephew of the man who shot her Dean was trying to chase her off their farm. It wasn't right.

Ida didn't like fighting—a total waste of valuable time as far as she was concerned—but she could when provoked. If Campbell kept pushing, she'd take the fight to him.

She gritted her teeth. No sweet-talking con man was going to talk her out of what was hers—no matter how much gold he dangled in front of her. No strategically placed bullet was going to scare her away.

Raising a fist, she shouted defiantly into the night sky, "You just try, Beau Campbell. I haven't survived this unforgiving land by being meek."

* * * *

At that moment, Jared Buell stepped onto his white-columned front porch wearing a silk dinner jacket. His East Coast-educated daughter had the fixed idea that a silk jacket was a necessary part of a wealthy man's evening attire. He willingly indulged his daughter. Kate was so much like her late mother where social conventions were concerned.

He took in deep breaths and flexed the kinks out of his

legs, one ear tuned to the crickets. If they stopped chirping, he'd be warned of someone approaching.

Jared's living was mainly supplying beef to the military. When he could, he captured and green broke wild horses to sell as cavalry mounts to Ft. Kearney soldiers. With Rattlesnake's nephew in town, he'd warned the wranglers to be on the alert for rustling. "Hard for a thief to keep his hands off another man's property," he muttered to himself.

For extra income, Jared sold hunting rights to the New York and Philadelphia millionaires who vacationed at hotels in Sheridan and Buffalo, and to the guests of Bill Cody's Wild West Show. Shining Mountains—the Indian name for the Big Horn Mountains—was a source of plentiful hunting and fishing.

He gazed at the snow-capped, ragged peaks outlined against the night sky. Snow melting from the nine thousand-foot mountain brought life-giving water to his ranch and to the foothills of graceful aspen and the meadows of native grasses. A harsh land, yet a land Jared owned with pride. Partridge, grouse and pheasant bedded down in the same meadows that elk, mountain lion and bear inhabited. They drank the same waters for life—yet fought to the death, becoming either food for survival or death on four legs.

If the Pinkerton report proved that Campbell's nephew was indeed his old enemy, he must find a way to stop the killer before he blended into this land to become—for Jared—death stalking on two legs.

Chapter 6

Wednesday morning, Ernest was digging into the hearty breakfast Peggy had placed on the kitchen table. "I pulled the carcass of a mule deer out of the pond near the upper creek."

Ida's stomach contracted. She knew her cousin had gone out early—even before the two hands were stirring—to make sure everything was quiet after Tuesday's shooting. Evidently, it wasn't.

"Where?"

"Near the Bar J," he said. "At first it looked natural. I only spotted the bullet hole when I had the horse drag it out. Would've tainted the creek."

Ida slipped into her seat and started dishing up a plate of breakfast.

Ernest sat near the farm hands. He spoke between mouthfuls. "It must've been thrown in last night after I brought the milk cows in."

Peggy added more flapjacks to the diminishing stack. "Bar J people responsible, do you think? It's near their land."

The field hand, Buck, spoke up. "Ain't likely. Not their nature. 'Sides, they would've used their end of the creek— just flung the carcass there. Wouldn't have known nothing was wrong 'til the animals got sick." He forked two more flapjacks onto his plate.

"Campbell...again, I bet." Resignation crept into her voice. "Rattlesnake never complains about the Bar J taking his water."

Ernest dripped black-strap molasses onto a new stack of steaming hot flapjacks. "The Bar J has a dozen regular hands on top of Jared and Russ and some mean-looking drifters. Campbell would be crazy to go up against that strong a force."

Ida wrinkled her brow, considering her options. "We need to work without worrying. I'd better ask the Mason boy to be a lookout. Todd can ride around and keep an eye out while we work."

"How will we pay him?" Ernest asked. "We already have two fulltime hands."

"I'll pay him in whatever canned vegetables and jellies his ma wants," Ida said. "We have enough from last harvest to share."

"Might work," Ernest said.

Peggy rinsed her hands under the pump and hung her apron on a hook before plopping down on a kitchen chair to dish up her breakfast. "I'll ride over to the Bar J this afternoon and talk to Todd and his ma and visit a while. Sadie and I swap recipes, you remember."

Ida envied the two women who'd so successfully mastered the art of low atmosphere cooking. With Buffalo at nearly five thousand feet above sea level, water boiled at a lower temperature, causing timing problems.

She'd planned to work in the barn after breakfast, but wondered if she should go with Peggy. It would appear unmannerly if she didn't get permission from Sadie's employer. Besides, she was interested to see Jared. Their animosity had cooled while fighting the fire. They might even have a chance to become friends.

Peggy took her empty plate to the sink. "Why don't I go upstairs and get dressed."

Ida pushed up from her chair, her mind made up. "I'll come with you. Our high and mighty neighbor might call me underhanded if I hire his tenant's son from under his nose without putting in an appearance."

She looked down at her stained trousers. "I'd better change and make a good impression. After all, I'm the one coming begging."

* * * *

Later that morning, Ida pulled the farm wagon to a halt on the road to the Bar J. She and Peggy were still too far away to see the ranch house, but they didn't need to go farther. Jared Buell was cantering toward them on a black gelding. The rancher looked impressive in his banker's clothes of pin-striped pants and black frock coat—like a statesman. A warm flush of awareness in an attractive male flowed through Ida and her blood heated. She had no defenses to stop it.

"Good morning, Mr. Buell. May we have a moment of your time?"

He drew up beside the wagon and doffed his hat, sitting

effortlessly on the tooled leather saddle. "You caught me on my way to the bank for a board meeting. What may I do for you?"

"You know we've been having troubles on the farm since Art Campbell's nephew came to stay."

Ida saw Buell's immediate scowl and wondered what on earth she'd said with these few words to make him react like that. "Someone shot at Ernest and me while we were planting, and this morning a gunshot deer was thrown in the pond that our cattle use. We've come to ask permission to hire Todd Mason to keep an eye out while we work."

Another scowl deepened the weathered lines on his face.

"I'm not his parent. You'll have to ask his mother."

He spit out the words as if they were bullets and she was the target. Steel gray eyes bored into her, unsettling her. He wasn't making this easy. She swallowed. Strangely, despite her increasing irritation with the man, she had an urge to tuck back a lock of dark hair peppered with gray that had fallen over one eye when he'd doffed his hat.

"We're on our way to Sadie now." Ida feared she'd start stuttering from the tension she felt between them. "I wanted to be sure you had no objection since they live on your ranch."

He tightened his hands on the reins and his shoulders visibly stiffened. Disapproval flowed out of him. "I do object. Campbell is dangerous. Todd shouldn't be put in the middle of things."

This is why they never got along. No give in the man. After all, she wasn't planning a range war. She just wanted to get on with her planting without having to look over her shoulder.

"I'm still willing to buy you out," he said. "Campbell wouldn't pull that stuff on me."

Ida pulled herself upright and squared her shoulders. "I'm not selling. And I'll not be driven out."

Jared scowled once again and she assumed he was worried about the boy.

"We'll not ask Todd to do anything dangerous. If he spots anything, he comes and tells us. We'll take care of the trouble ourselves."

"He's worked for us before, you remember," Peggy said. "He knows the lay of the land—how to get around, what to watch out for."

He didn't look convinced. Ida decided to act anyway and raised her chin. "Sorry to bother you. We'd best speak to his mother."

Her voice sounded haughty even to her own ears. She flicked the reins, telling Old Molly, "Walk on."

As the wagon pulled away, she took one last look back. Her stomach knotted at the fury she saw on Jared's face.

* * * *

Later that evening, Jared was in his ranch office with Russ, having just finished scrutinizing the accounts. He'd resisted his daughter's attempts to get him to dress for dinner and had changed banker's clothes for a plaid flannel shirt with the sleeves rolled up.

His commodious office and his equally large bedroom were the rooms at the ranch where he felt most at ease. The roll-top office desk and matching oak table and chairs had been bought at auction from the railroad and refinished locally. A friend had crafted the soft leather sofa and two side chairs. A variety of well-worn books lined the east wall of the office, butting up against pigeonholes and shelves with metal containers to protect ranch records. The bedroom was dominated by an extra long walnut carved bed and matching wardrobe. The rest of the rooms were decorated to the taste of his socially conscious mother-in-law and daughter. Too frilly for his taste.

"Someone put a dead deer in Osterbach water the other morning," Russ said as he stored away the account ledgers.

Jared scowled and ran fingers through his graying hair. "She hired Todd Mason to be a lookout. I think it's a bad idea."

"Not to Sadie. She feels her son can handle himself."

"We'll see."

If Campbell was the Kansas outlaw, Todd might be in extreme danger. Jared had checked for a telegram from the Pinkertons when he was in town, but there was nothing. It could be months before he'd know for a certainty about Beau's background.

"They'll get plenty of good cooking out of it," Russ said. "Sadie said it would be a blessing to eat someone else's canning for a change."

Jared grimaced. "Seems everything has a silver lining."

Russ' eyes narrowed. "Boss, I know Ida Osterbach rubs you the wrong way, but give her some credit. It took courage to stand up to Rattlesnake's nephew."

Jared shifted uncomfortably in his chair. He knew that to Russ you were the sum of your deeds—woman or man.

"I'll admit she's got guts." That was her trouble, too many mannish qualities—although he'd been surprised this morning by how nice Ida looked in a dress.

"Intelligent, too," Russ added.

Jared looked askance at his foreman. "How do you figure that?"

"Peggy said she finished tenth grade back east. She reads Latin and the classics for fun."

That was interesting. Jared had enjoyed those family times when Isabella read aloud to him in the evenings.

"She has a big dose of common sense, too," Russ said. "She runs that farm for a profit."

"Hmmm."

"She's a survivor."

Russ was getting on Jared's nerves. A stabbing pain traveled along his brow. He ran his fingers across the pain to massage it away. Although it was six years since Isabella's death, he still carried guilt for dragging his petite, cultured wife to Wyoming. If they'd moved East after the Kansas tragedy, she might still be alive. The influenza that took her was only the means to her death. The root cause was not being able to adapt, not being strong enough for the frontier.

He'd supplied what luxuries he could afford as he built his spread. He even took her to Buffalo and Sheridan for weeks at a time to mix with the vacationing rich. Nothing was enough. Isabella craved a city life he despised. And he was out chasing that outlaw when she took ill and died. The guilt that he hadn't been at her side haunted him.

Ida survived the frontier. His sweet Isabella had not.

His gut twisted. One more bone of contention with that farmer woman.

* * * *

Two days later, Beau Campbell sat with his uncle on the shaded front porch as the sky darkened, their chairs tilted against the weathered wall. Diablo Avilos lolled on the porch step, his back against a post, his sombrero tilted over his scarred face. A cricket was singing close at hand. Diablo moved lightning fast to stomp on it.

"That damn farmer woman is a pain in the ass," Beau said.

"Her *pinche* hands carry guns these days," Diablo said.

"Heared she hired Widder Mason's boy ta' be her eyes and ears." Art spat tobacco juice off the front porch.

"She's slowing down my plans," Beau spoke through gritted teeth.

"*Revancha?*" Diablo asked lazily.

"It's too early for revenge," Beau said. "I'm trying first to convince the good folks of Buffalo that I'm solid citizenry." In his mind's eye, he already saw himself as a gentleman rancher. He wouldn't let anyone stand in the way of that dream.

Art snorted. "Won't get 'em on yer side."

Beau bristled, resenting his uncle's lack of faith. One day he was going to shut that old man up.

"I did in Missouri. They reverenced me there." While still a shadowy leader of a Kansas outlaw gang riding under an assumed name, he'd established a reputable way of life in the neighboring state under his true name. Capitalizing on the veneer of polite southern ways instilled by his mother, he'd become—if not a pillar of the community—at least an acceptable member of its society. "Only, I flirted with one too many married women. I won't make that mistake again."

"That woman needs to be hit where it hurts most," his uncle said as he chewed his cud, "—in her pocketbook."

That could be done. But it couldn't be straight forward like robbing trains. It must be subtle.

With a crash, his chair's legs slammed to the floor boards. Beau's cunning mind had come up with a scheme. A smug grin wiped the snarl from his face.

"Great idea, Uncle Art.

Chapter 7

Mid-morning the next day, Beau sauntered into the elegant Occidental Hotel dining room. He'd been told that for years this Buffalo hotel hosted most of the political, social and cultural gatherings of Johnson County. He absorbed the subdued hustle and bustle as if it could become a layer of skin—important people making important decisions. And making money while doing it.

I may run for office myself, he decided. *I'll get my hands on some of that graft.*

His eyes scanned the tables with their linen cloths and porcelain tea services until he saw a flighty, but rich girl he'd met the other day. She was having early morning tea with two older women. He doffed his hat and made a bee line for their table. Here was an opportunity to get in good with society matrons.

"Is this not the most fortunate of meetings, Miss Dawson?" Beau raised her outstretched hand to his lips. "Once again, my day is brightened by seeing your lovely face."

"Why, Mr. Campbell," she cooed, "how unexpected to see you in town again so soon." She waved a hand toward the oldest woman, "May I introduce Mrs. Evans to you. She's the grandmother of my dearest friend."

He bowed. "Charmed, I'm sure."

She waved a hand toward the woman beside her. "You've met my companion?"

The hired help, he thought. They needed charming, too. He bowed to the woman.

"I've not had the immense pleasure." He looked back toward Gertrude Dawson to say, "You were with your most beautiful mother when we made our acquaintanceship last week. It was obvious at that encounter where you got your beauty."

Looking delighted, she blushed before turning to her companions. "May I introduce Mr. Beaufort Campbell. He's taking over the management of his uncle's ranch out where the south road goes to the old fort. His Uncle Art is retiring."

"Beau to my friends," he said smoothly, even though he thought he saw Mrs. Evans' nose rise in disdain when his uncle's name was mentioned. It might take more effort than he'd planned to soften up the society matrons.

"Do join us, Mr. Campbell." Mrs. Evans' voice was cool, but polite. The matriarch pulled off a regal look even while her gray hair was rolled and pinned under a ridiculous hat that looked suitable for a bird's nest.

"Don't mind if I do." Beau pulled up an empty chair.

"I've just taken bouquets of flowers to the church for tomorrow's service," the woman said. "I was fortunate enough to meet up with Miss Dawson and her companion when I dropped by the hotel for a cup of tea."

Beau saw they were almost done with the cakes. He needed to keep this tea party going if he wanted enough time to make an impression and to make sure he was seen by enough people. He put his Stetson on a spare table next to them before asking, "May I order more sweets?"

"Not another bite for me," Miss Dawson said.

Mrs. Evans waved a hand in dismissal.

The companion shook her head.

"What was I thinking?" he said in mock horror. "Ladies such as yourselves must keep a watchful eye on trim waistlines."

The Dawson girl giggled.

The waiter set a place for him and poured his tea. Beau hated trying to get his fingers around the tiny handle on these porcelain tea cups. He'd have to be careful not to snap one off. He raised his cup in a gesture of salute. "Morning tea with charming ladies is by far profitable to the errands I'd planned today."

Actually, he was in town to establish an alibi.

"You're quite well dressed for errands, Mr. Campbell." Mrs. Evans looked at his red paisley vest and gray frockcoat as if she didn't quite approve.

He was determined to be charming if it killed him. "One never knows when a lucky opportunity will come along to chat with refined ladies."

"We're the fortunate ones, to have found so amiable a male companion for our morning tea." Gertrude leaned evocatively toward him and patted his hand.

He hated the phoniness of her airs and feigned seduction. Beau preferred the earthy truthfulness of whores.

They spent the next hour chatting about performances by the opera touring company which had been at the theatre last week. He compared their performance against those he attended in Kansas and Missouri. They then went on and on about the difficulty of getting the latest fashions in a small town like Buffalo.

As a small boy, his mother had put him through many an afternoon tea with boring women fawning over him. He was forced to sit quietly in his Sunday best clothes and smile politely and listen to this same kind of inconsequential chatter. Those sessions were good practice for getting in good with Buffalo's society matrons.

Beau smiled steadily. He resisted grinding his teeth.

* * * *

Ida was regretting her impulse this morning to drive the farm wagon to Buffalo. The closer it got to the noon hour, the hotter it was becoming. She wiped sweat off her forehead with the back of her sleeve. She gritted her teeth and kept on going. It would take at least another half hour to get to the livery station and give the old horse and herself a rest away from this unforgiving sun.

To build store credit for the farm during the lean winter months, Ida sold the excess crops to a store owned by friends. Established on Main Street, this mercantile store had grown from an early tent store until it sold any item a Buffalo resident might need. Usually, Ernest drove the wagon of sale goods on Saturday and brought back the supplies. This morning, Ida decided to be wagoner because she wanted to look over bolts of fabric that Ernest said had arrived at the store last week.

The mare knew exactly where to go. It did this trek on Saturdays and often on Sundays for church. Ida was half drowsing with only a light grip on the reins when she was startled fully alert. Two masked riders appeared from behind a rock outcropping, shooting into the air as if to scare the horse and make it bolt. Ida gathered the reins more securely. Her heart leapt to her throat. She couldn't get away. There was no extra speed to be had from Old Molly. She reached down to unlatch the lid of the storage box under the wagon's seat to get at the loaded shotgun.

Seeing the mare wouldn't bolt, the men rammed their horses against the side of the laden, unstable wagon, urging their mounts to push it over. Ida gave up reaching for the shotgun. The wagon rocked dangerously from side to side. She flung herself across the wooden seat and struggled to use her weight against the side tilting off the ground.

Merciful heaven! she thought. *All our hard work. It'll be trampled into the dirt.*

Her heart pounded and her breathing increased threefold.

Ignoring the sweat droplets running freely down her face, she fought to use her weight to counterbalance the men's attempts to tip the wagon. The horses already had raised the wheels on one side of the wagon slightly off the roadway. One of the men reached down and pushed at her shoulder, trying to make her lose her grip.

"Get away from me," she cried out. "Help!"

She tried to bite his hand while she clung to the wagon's side.

From the corner of her sweat-stung eye, Ida saw four

riders galloping toward her from the direction of Buffalo.

Oh, dear Lord! she thought. *Don't let that be more of them!*

One of the masked men spotted the riders and grunted. "Let's git."

Good. No friends of these bastards.

Wagon wheels thumped onto the packed-dirt roadway when the men turned their horses away. They raked their boots along their mounts' sides to urge them into a gallop.

With the wagon safely on four wheels, relief poured through Ida. "Whoa," she said, but Molly had already stopped. She wrapped the reins around the wagon's post, grabbed the shotgun from the box and sent a spray of buckshot after the men. Too far away.

Her heart—while still pumping rapidly—was slowing down.

She jumped down to check the horse. Patting down the mare's body, she looked for sore spots or gashes. Finding none, she checked the leather leads. Twisted, but she quickly straightened them out. She was checking the wagon, shotgun in hand, when the first of the four riders pulled up alongside.

"You all right, Ma'am?" he called out. "We heared gunshots."

"I am now." She recognized him as a wrangler from the Bar J ranch. She stored the shotgun under the seat before she said, "If you hadn't come along, I don't know how I'd have ended up. Probably sprawled in that ditch under a pile of my farm goods." She rocked her head to the side to indicate the deepest ditch.

Jared was one of the other four riders. He rode up to her and reined in his gelding. "Did you recognize them?"

She shook her head. "They wore masks, and I didn't know the horses. But when they rode off, they high-tailed it towards the Campbell ranch."

Jared swore. "Begging your pardon, Ma'am." He touched his hat in respect.

"No use chasin' 'em," the wrangler observed. "Got too much head start."

A tremor rolled through her as she calmed Molly with long strokes along its side. "This horse deserves an extra ration of oats. They couldn't shake her."

"How much produce did you lose?" Jared asked.

"I don't know. I'll have to look."

Her check of the wagon revealed no damage other than a few broken eggs that had spilled out of a tipped basket. "A few eggs."

"You was lucky," the wrangler said.

"Don't I know it! This wagon load represents a week's work. If you hadn't come along..." She left the sentence unfinished.

Strangely, now that it was over, she found herself trembling violently—so much so that her teeth chattered. When the wrangler offered to help her into the wagon, she accepted. Her legs were weak.

"Don't yer worry none, Ma'am," he said as he settled her onto the seat. "We'll foller you to town to make sure they don't try nothin'." He handed her the reins she'd wrapped around the wagon post.

"Shorty," Jared said, "you get up there and take those reins."

"Sure, boss." Shortly tied his horse to the back and climbed nimbly onto the wagon.

"Much obliged." Ida wiped the sweat from her forehead. "That took a lot out of me. I'm not my usual self."

"Try not to worry. We'll take care of you from here on in."

With that small act of kindness, Jared melted a wedge from the icy disdain lodged in her heart since their dispute over the hiring of Todd.

* * * *

Beau spotted the Osterbach wagon soon after he left the Occidental. It was maneuvering slowly along Main Street with a Bar J hand at the reins. The female farmer huddled with her arms wrapped around herself, but otherwise looked unharmed. The same with her farm goods. Worse yet, his nemesis rode alongside the wagon.

What a disaster.

He ducked into an alleyway.

Raging fury consumed him. The two men he'd sent were supposed to be dependable—men who got a job done. Why had they failed? He'd get answers before the sun set.

Beau had intended to spend more time in Buffalo in conversation with the prominent citizens—promoting good will. But he couldn't with his nemesis so close. Instead, he had to get out of town—fast—before Buell spotted him. He must navigate back alleys to get to his horse.

Like ten years ago, he'd sneak out with his tail between his legs. Rage flared.

The ignominy of it drove one more nail into Buell's casket.

Chapter 8

Early that evening, Ernest was sitting in the high-backed rocking chair on the front porch, listening to the increasing volume of the crickets. His lightweight, cotton shirt was unbuttoned down the front to give access to the coolness after the heat of the day. As his farsighted gaze roamed the horizon, he caught dark shadows moving slowly along the road.

Ida, returning from Buffalo.

There was a tall rider next to the wagon, but the rider peeled off and headed across the meadow toward the Bar J long before Ernest could make out who he was. It wasn't until his cousin had tied the mare at the water trough by the barn and was slowly walking toward him that he realized something was wrong. She sank down onto the porch step as if her knees could no longer hold her.

"You look like you wrestled with the devil."

"A devil named Beau Campbell," she answered.

Ernest came alert. "What happened?"

"Just outside Buffalo, two masked men rode from behind boulders and shot off guns, trying to scare Old

Molly and wreck the wagon."

"Son-of-a-gun!" He leaned forward, tilting the rocker dangerously, and squeezed his hands into fists. "Are you hurt?"

She shook her head. "They weren't trying to shoot me. They wanted to scare our horse into bolting and wrecking the wagon. It would've trashed a whole week of our work."

"Holy cow!"

"They didn't know how little bothers Old Molly. That mare just kept plodding along."

The relief Ernest felt went beyond words. He raked his fingers through his thick, blond hair. "When I get my hands on those bastards..."

"I didn't recognize them. I didn't know their horses, either."

"How did you get away?"

"Some Bar J riders were on the road ahead of me. They heard the gunshots and turned back."

"Did they catch them?"

She shook her head. "The shooters high-tailed it before the Bar J men got to me. I'm assuming Beau Campbell was behind this, but I have no proof."

Ernest was just as glad they'd skedaddled. Ida didn't need to be caught in the middle of a gunfight. "Who was that riding alongside just now?"

"Jared Buell. He insisted I shouldn't come home alone."

Ernest grinned. "Buell?"

Ida looked sheepish. "As shaky as I'm feeling, I was grateful."

Ernest pushed himself up out of the rocking chair and

held out a hand to his cousin for support. "Come inside and get your supper. You look like you could use some strong coffee."

She dragged herself slowly to her feet. "What about Old Molly?"

"I'll get Hank to take care of her. And the wagon and the supplies."

"Have him give her an extra ration of oats. She deserves it."

* * * *

Ida followed Ernest, her feet lagging from exhaustion and her body aching as if it had been fed through a thrasher. The only good things about today were the bolts of colorful fabric nestling among the supplies in the wagon.

Ernest led the way to the kitchen where she sank into a chair, her stomach growling from the aroma of mutton stew heating on the stove. She retold her story several times. Peggy fussed over her and made her eat a bowl of stew.

Todd—still seated at the dinner table feasting on a stack of biscuits—piped up. "Miz Osterbach, you oughta ask Mr. Buell for help. He's got lots of tough men working for him."

"Thanks, Todd, but I don't like to be beholden."

"Asking for a little help isn't weakness, my friend," Peggy assured her. "It's just another way of taking care of the farm."

"Most times we rub each other the wrong way," Ida answered.

"That can't be," Todd said. "He's too nice. And he could use a good woman like you. His daughter and mother-in-law ain't fit company. Too prissy."

Peggy laughed delightedly. "There you go, my friend. Ask for help and get a marriage proposal at the same time."

Ernest chuckled.

Ida flushed. "Just stop!"

"Talk has it," the farm hand, Buck, said, turning the conversation away from its focus on her, "that Buell had a run in with Beau Campbell years ago. Serious."

"I heard that, too," Ernest spoke around a mouthfull of food.

"He telegraphed the Pinkertons about it last week, they say," Buck added.

Peggy scraped the last of the stew into a bowl. "He'd help if you asked. He helped you today."

"Well, I'm not asking," Ida declared emphatically. "Forget about it."

She didn't like seeming incapable of handling her own problems. She'd fallen apart today when the wagon was attacked. Buell must think little enough of her already—let alone what he'd think if she went begging for more help. She squared her shoulders. "I've taken care of this farm since Dean's been gone and I'll keep on doing it."

Her stubbornness must've been obvious because they dropped their objections.

Ida felt considerably less weary now that she had solid food and strong coffee in her stomach. "When I told Herman Gentry what happened, he decided to send his own wagon out here each Saturday."

"No one would dare bother the store's wagon, would they?" Peggy said.

"Did Herman talk about cost?" Ernest asked.

"Wouldn't take a nickel," Ida replied, "but I think we should throw in some extras each week. That way we're not beholden."

"I could send baked goods." Peggy wiped her hands with a moist rag. "I've wanted to sell in town, you know, but never got around to it."

Todd smacked his lips. "They'll like that."

Peggy grinned at the teenager and ruffled his hair. He blushed and ducked away.

"Between paying Todd and paying the store, we're liable to be short ourselves," Ida pointed out.

"Can't be helped," Peggy said. "Herman and Martha are good friends to do this."

"It'll save wear and tear on Old Molly," Buck added.

Ida carried dirty dishes to the sink.

"Will they just send the wagon each week," Ernest asked, "or will we have to let them know when to send it?"

"Every Saturday—unless we get word to them. I already gave them a list of staples we'd need. We'll have to send a note for anything extra we want."

"This'll show those Campbells we have friends who stand by us," Ida said.

Chapter 9

Jared was trying to figure out why Todd Mason was hanging around the ranch house on a glorious spring day. Todd had sat close at church that morning and now was lingering inside. Usually, he was out fishing or hunting on a Sunday. On top of that, he was still wearing his Sunday-best clothing and looking uncomfortable. "Something on your mind, Todd?"

"As a matter of fact, Mr. Buell, there is. I've been doin' some work for Miz Osterbach."

The muscles between Jared's shoulder blades tightened. "So I heard."

"She's havin' trouble from Art Campbell's nephew. He shot at her and her cousin when they were plantin', then left a dead animal to rot in her pond."

"So she told me."

"Just yesterday, he sent two men to spook her horse and tip over the wagon when she was driving their butchered meat into town."

"I know. My wranglers and I drove the men off. What's your point, Todd?"

"Shucks, Mr. Buell." Todd fidgeted in his seat with a hangdog expression. "She could use your help."

Jared wanted to tell his young tenant to mind his own business. Instead, he forced himself to answer politely, "If she needs help, she should ask me herself—not send you."

Todd's head shot up. "She'd be madder than a hornet if she knew I was askin'. She truly is stubborn. But she's such a nice lady. I don't like to see her hurt."

Hardly a lady, Jared thought. *She wears breeches.*

"Jumping Jehosaphat, Mr. Buell. Beau Campbell's mean. I keep an eye out, but—"

Jared interrupted him. "You're taking care of her already. She doesn't need me." He had enough problems without taking on those of a woman who was far from helpless. "You keep doing your job, Todd, and keep your nose out of mine."

"But Mr. Buell…"

Jared decided to throw the boy a bone—something he already had in mind.

"Tell you what, Todd. I'll send to town to get the telegraph agent to find out where the sheriff got himself off to. We'll warn him about the trouble between Campbell and Osterbach. Tell him to get himself back here. I'll even contact the U.S. Marshal. He's a friend of mine and should be glad of an excuse to visit."

Todd's grin was wide.

"But if that woman wants more help," Jared added, "she can come to the ranch and beg me herself."

The grin faded.

* * * *

In the cool of that evening, Beau and his uncle were smoking on the ranch house porch. Art moved slowly on the rocking chair, creating a rhythmic squeak as he rocked. Beau lounged against a porch support beam. Diablo Avilos lay stretched out underneath a nearby shade tree, chewing a wide blade of grass.

"That farmer woman has the magical luck of the Irish," Beau was saying.

"What'er the odds those Bar J men 'ud show up?" his uncle commiserated.

"The store's sending its wagon," Diablo said.

"Can't mess wit' the store." Art spoke around a chew of tobacco. "We buy from 'em."

"Don't intend to."

"*¡Pendejo!* Stop being so damned nice." Diablo batted at a pesky fly, catching it and squeezing it in his palm.

Beau thought for a while before answering. "You might be right, my friend. I've been holding back because I want to get a better footing in town with the social set."

Art took a long drag on his cigarette and blew a puff of smoke before speaking. "What about 'em wimen ya' met? Can you use 'em to get inta high society?"

"Maybe. The girl has feathers for brains, but her industrialist father's a bigwig. It might help me to court her."

"What about the older *puta*?" Diablo asked.

"Mrs. Evans? She unthawed a bit, but mostly kept her nose in the air."

His uncle stopped rocking and looked alert. "Evans?"

Puzzled at his reaction, Beau said, "Yeah."

"What's she look like?"

"Early sixties, a small woman, gray hair, a ridiculous hat with flowers on it."

His uncle rocked backward in the chair and laughed. "You was havin' tea with Buell's mother-in-law!"

Diablo guffawed.

Beau's shoulders tensed and his mind grappled with the thought. "She never said."

"She is," his uncle insisted.

"I almost vomited from their endless gabbing." Beau mimicked the women in a high, squeaky voice. "Clothes this. The theater that." He turned to look at Art. "I was trying to butter up the Dawson girl. I didn't talk much with the old lady."

His uncle chewed on his cigarette before speaking. "Did she figger out who you was? Did ya know she lived with 'em in Kansas?"

"Shit. This gets worse and worse."

"Shoot 'em all and be done with it," Diablo said.

Beau would gladly put a bullet between her eyes if he could get away with it.

"Can't, *amigo*. I'm supposed to be the good citizen. I'll have to come up with another solution."

* * * *

Jared relaxed in the parlor after dinner that Sunday night, listening to his raven-haired daughter play classical music on their upright piano. Her pearl-toned skin glowed translucently in the flickering light of the oil lamp, reminding him heartbreakingly of her mother. They were alone, his mother-in-law having gone to bed early.

Since her return in December from an East Coast finishing school, Kate dressed formally each evening. Tonight she wore a jacket cut to a point at the back, emphasizing a waist as slim as her mother's. Its black, taffeta skirt had too many ruffles for his taste, but then, Jared never truly understood the interests of females. He'd contentedly worshipped Isabella from afar, rather than get mired in her complexities.

Jared had paid good money to that finishing school and had gotten a daughter who felt herself better than almost everyone else in Buffalo. But his mother-in-law was pleased. A true lady, Kate's grandmother described her. An educated snob, Jared countered affectionately. From one corner of his mind, he heard, *"Father."*

Kate used the formal "Father" these days instead of her childhood "Papa." It was a wonder she hadn't addressed him in French, which she was prone to do.

"People are talking about the arrival in town of Art Campbell's nephew." Kate played the piano while she spoke, without missing a note. "Grandmama met him this morning at the Occidental."

Jared froze. When he didn't respond, Kate turned slightly to look at him.

"Mon père? Ecouté moi?"

"I heard you, sweetheart." His stomach churned. "I'm trying to find a refined way to say this, but I can't. I believe the man's a no-good, lying, murdering bastard. Stay away from him."

"Father!" Kate's mouth bowed with shock. She stopped playing and swiveled on the piano stool to glare at him. "That can't be true! Not from what grandmama said. She said he was most charming, although he misuses words."

Jared shifted uneasily on the satin wing chair. He wasn't absolutely sure Beau was his brother's killer. The Pinkerton report would settle matters once it got here. In the meantime, Kate needed to know his suspicions—he needed to protect her.

"Sugar, I believe the man now calling himself Beau Campbell was the leader of the outlaw gang that robbed Uncle Robert's bank."

"Merciful heavens!"

He could see the uncertainty on her face.

"Your Aunt Rose was waiting in the bank lobby while my brother closed the bank. They were going to the hotel for supper. The robbers pushed their way in and both died in the shoot-out. Rose was pregnant." As it had done many times over the years, his heart twisted in pain when he recalled that day.

A pout mixed with Kate's shock. "You always said they died of influenza." She almost whispered the words.

He nodded. "Your mother and I wanted to protect you."

"Still…you should have…"

Kate's canary chose that moment to burst into song from its cage, creating an incongruous contrast to the gravity of the conversation.

"As a little girl, I always wondered why we stopped seeing Aunt Rose." She sounded sad. "I liked her. Then we moved away and Mama said they both got sick and passed on."

"You were so young…"

"Tell me now," she said.

He sat on the piano stool with her and held her hand as

he told her the story. He left out how Isabella was frantic to save her daughter from the violence that hit so close to home and insisted on moving. The only reason her mother gave up pushing the idea of moving East was that, even with the inheritance from his brother, they didn't have enough money to live in style in an East Coast city. In a small town like Buffalo, which hosted the rich and powerful coming to Wyoming to vacation and hunt, he and his wife rose to the elite of town society. They easily mingled with the powerful during their Wyoming stay. It had been enough for Isabella for a while.

He ended his explanation to Kate with, "I rode with the Kansas posse that chased them down. Everyone but the leader was killed. He got away, wounded, but he had to leave the bank gold behind. Robert's portion of that money built this ranch. The rest bought shares in the bank."

Kate slowly shook her head, disbelief engraved on her face. "That outlaw doesn't sound anything like the mannerly gentleman Gertrude described."

His daughter took her hand back.

"She was impressed with him," Kate said resolutely.

"Gertrude Dawson doesn't have the brains she was born with." Jared could feel his dander rising just thinking about his daughter being influenced by that dim-witted female. "Any smooth talker could convince her he was born a prince."

Her chin rose and trembled slightly. "Father...she's a dear friend."

"That doesn't make her less of an imbecile."

There was an edge to Kate's voice. "But she said he

was fascinating. She said he was a good-looking man with rough edges."

Jared became afraid Kate believed her friend. "He's a smooth-tongued son-of-a-bitch, pardon my French. A dozen years ago, he pulled the wool over the eyes of the Kansas women with his good looks."

"Grandmama said he was gentlemanly and could even discuss the opera. He had attended several in Missouri."

"I believe he's no good."

"I'm sure I can discern these things for myself." Kate's voice was icy. "I was taught how to take the measure of everyone I meet."

His anger rising several notches, he glared at his beautiful daughter. "Stay away from him. If he is who I think he is, he's extremely dangerous."

Kate looked insulted. She sniffed and pulled herself upright, her chin held high.

"I never planned to socialize with him. No matter what Gertrude says about how handsome and charming he is, he's not on our social level. His uncle's ranch is small and dilapidated."

For once Jared was relieved his daughter was a snob like her mother.

Chapter 10

Late morning on Monday, the emergency bell by the kitchen door clanged. Ida's heart clenched and her stomach tumbled. *What now?*

She dropped her tools in the furrows, grabbed her shotgun and ran, covered in dirt and heart pounding. As she got close to the farmhouse, she saw that everyone had rushed back from the fields in answer to the alarm. She made a point to stay well away from the clean laundry flapping on the clotheslines.

"What's up?" she shouted as she closed in on Peggy, who had worry lines ridging her face. She was on the back porch, gesturing to them to hurry.

"Indians on the road. In full war paint."

Not good. Indian renegades still occasionally made life uncomfortable. The farm was as ready for attack as it could be. As a rule, the farmhouse's wooden shutters—thick enough to withstand a fiery arrow or a barrage of bullets—stayed closed during the day when no one was in those rooms. Large, wooden barrels of rainwater were strategically placed around the farmhouse and outbuildings for fighting fires.

"I'll start closing up downstairs." Ernest passed Peggy and rushed into the farmhouse.

"Did that already," Peggy said.

Ida headed to the metal basin in the kitchen sink to wash the caked dirt off her hands so she'd have a good grip on the trigger.

Rifles and handguns already lay on the kitchen table where Peggy had been preparing the mid-day meal. Leftover peelings and food scraps had been discarded into a large bowl as swill for the hogs. The two hired hands grabbed pistols and ammunition and left for the barn to set up crossfire positions. Their heavy work boots raised dust as they ran across the barnyard. Ernest barred the kitchen door behind them.

Ida's shoulders stiffened with tension. Her heartbeat increased. Although the farmhouse was built for defense, there was always a chance the attackers would win.

She and Ernest checked the guns for a full load while Peggy pumped an extra bucket of water as a precaution against fires. The room was hushed except for the sounds of their preparations. After dropping extra shells into the deep recesses of her pants pocket, Ida abandoned the kitchen and took up a firing position by the front door.

Opening its porthole, she peered out, puzzled why Indians would threaten her farm and why they were taking their time about attacking. Years before, she and Dean had nursed injured Sioux. Lately, Peggy traded home-cooked meals for beaded Crow jackets, blankets and leather moccasins. Until now, Indians had respected the farm. It was more than unsettling to see four on her road in full war gear.

"They're too far away. I can't see which tribe," Ida said as Peggy and Ernest joined her.

"I'll get the spyglass," he replied.

The Indians were sitting quietly on their horses, but Ida knew Indians often appeared calm before violent attacks.

A few minutes later, Ernest returned from the parlor with the spyglass and looked through the porthole. He made some lens adjustments and burst out laughing. "You know who that is?"

"Who?" Peggy asked.

"That's Long Wolf. Buffalo Bill must be back in Sheridan."

Friends, not marauders.

Relief swept through Ida and her racing heart slowed down as she rested her rifle alongside the doorjamb. She sent Peggy out to the barn to tell the farm hands that everything was all right and to invite them back into the kitchen for their mid-day meal. She unbarred the heavy wooden door, stepped out onto the front porch and waved to her war-painted friend and his three companions.

The four Indians spurred their horses and galloped toward the farmhouse, whooping and waving tomahawks, just like in their Wild West Shows. Dust clouded the air as their horses came to a stop in clouds of dust.

Ida was laughing. "Greetings, Chief Long Wolf. Showing off?"

"Why the war paint?" Ernest asked as the Indians dismounted and tied their festooned mustangs to the hitching rail. One of them pumped water into the trough for the horses as the others walked toward the front porch.

"You scared us to death." Ida chided her friend. "We thought you were renegades on the war path."

"That's why we took our time." Chief Long Wolf shook hands all around. "Didn't want to be shot."

He introduced Sioux Chiefs Flies Above, Rocky Bear and American Horse, also members of Buffalo Bill Cody's Wild West Show. Although Long Wolf was the shortest of the four Indians, his demeanor and powerful build spoke of his preeminence.

"Europeans hire us to hunt," Rocky Bear explained. "Cody say dress in war gear. Experience the Old West." His expression was resigned, yet contemptuous of the vagaries of show business.

Each wore feathered headdresses cascading down their backs, with long-sleeved leather garments and beaded moccasins on their feet. Flies Above and American Horse wore bone breastplates, while Rocky Bear wore a necklace of silver disks hanging down past his waistline. Long Wolf had draped a fox pelt around his neck. Although tomahawks and war mallets had been left with the horses, each carried a wicked-looking knife in a sheath attached to a braided belt.

"Where are the Europeans?" Ida asked. "Abandoned in the woods?"

"At Occidental, drinking champagne."

It was well known that Buffalo's Occidental Hotel hosted many famous travelers like Buffalo Bill Cody, Calamity Jane and General Sheridan. Rooms were expensive, two dollars fifty a day, but meals were served around the clock. The locals frequented its expensive dining room, billiards hall and barbershop. When Dean was alive, Ida used to have Sunday meal there after church.

She suggested they go to the kitchen. "You can eat while we catch up on gossip. Peggy made a delicious stew from some rabbits Ernest trapped. She baked fresh biscuits, too."

Long Wolf and his friends followed Ida. As they entered the kitchen, Ernest was removing the ammunition from the table and putting the guns away in the sideboard.

"Glad I didn't rush in," Long Wolf said when he saw what Ernest was doing.

"I told you." Ida's pulse was now back to normal. "You gave us a scare."

The farmhands and Peggy were introduced to Long Wolf's friends.

Peggy laid out plates and utensils while Buck got some chairs from the parlor and Ernest disappeared outside to wash up in the trough. The men pulled out chairs to sit at the table—the Indians getting the places of honor nearest Ida. Peggy was dishing up the aromatic stew from the large metal pot kept simmering on the wood stove by the time Ernest came back inside. She finished putting out biscuits, butter and jam. Ida looked around the table, content with the friendship she saw. Hank and Buck vowed to the Sioux that someday they would get enough money to attend a Wild West Show.

"We get you in for free," Flies Above promised them.

"Yahoo," Buck howled.

As they were finishing their meal, Chief Long Wolf said he'd heard at the Occidental about Ida's troubles.

"How much do you know?" She reached for another biscuit. Long Wolf started explaining. By the time he finished, Ida was flabbergasted. "Word gets around, doesn't it?"

Chief American Horse grinned. "Gossip travels fast as prairie drums."

"How we help?" Rocky Bear asked.

"Been a while since had good fight," American Horse said at the same time.

"Remember how make smoke-signals like I show you?" Long Wolf asked.

Ida nodded energetically, her mouth full of food.

"Need us, light fire. We come. We around maybe two months," American Horse said. "Then go east for show."

"I'll lay out a fire today," Ida said after swallowing.

"I do it." Flies Above rose to his feet. "Where kindling?"

Ernest led Flies Above out the kitchen door to prepare a signal fire. Ida urged the last of the rabbit stew on her guests.

While they were gone, Peggy asked Long Wolf about their friends, Annie and Frank Butler. Ida always enjoyed hearing about Annie Oakley's adventures. She'd learned a lot about guns from her friend.

A short while later, the Indians headed back to the Occidental Hotel. That night, they had a war dance to perform for the Europeans.

"Signal us. Make your enemy pay," Long Wolf said.

The fierce-looking, war-painted men galloped toward Buffalo. Buck remarked, "I'm glad they're on our side."

* * * *

Late that afternoon, Russ Quentin approached. His boots resounded on the uncarpeted floor. Jared was reading through a stack of papers on the oak desk in his ranch office. He put a finger on the spot where he ended and twisted in his arm chair to look up at Russ.

"Troubles, boss. A couple dozen head of cattle are missing from the north range near the Osterbach farm."

"It's probably Campbell trying to make trouble between us. I hear a lot of unsavory characters are arriving at Art's ranch."

Russ nodded.

"They're getting drunk in town. Causing trouble."

Jared was uneasy. Beau was said to be all smiles and courtly charm when he was in Buffalo, but it seemed he couldn't control his uncivilized cohorts. Now, Beau made a direct move against him by stealing cattle.

"Do you know where they drove them?"

"Not yet. I've got our men out working on it."

"Good."

"What shall we do if we find them?"

"I'd say hang the thieving pack like in the old days, but we can't. Take them to the jail. The deputy will have to deal with them."

"Will do, boss."

Russ turned to leave and Jared settled back to his paperwork, but added over his shoulder, "I've telegraphed the sheriff and told him to get himself back to town. Trouble's brewing and that deputy's not decisive enough to handle it. I suspect we'll have to take care of this business ourselves until Angus gets back."

* * * *

The next morning, Jared's daughter cornered him in his office. He looked up, disturbed by the unexpected intrusion. Kate was begging for more clothing money. "Even in a backwater place like Buffalo, a lady needs a complete wardrobe for any occasion."

"Buffalo isn't a backwater."

"It's no Denver. Or even a Sheridan. Even so, I need to look presentable."

He looked at her, questioningly. Her red gingham dress with the wide ruffle at the hem looked fine to him. His indulged daughter could probably wear a different dress every morning and afternoon for a week before repeating an outfit. "You don't wear all the clothes in your closet now."

At that moment, his mother-in-law came through the doorway with a sweep of skirts. "That banker is calling on Katherine next Saturday. He's taking us to an evening of musical entertainment. She needs something new."

"Is Frank Larson considered an occasion to dress up?" Jared thought the intellectual banker too mild-mannered for his spirited daughter. She'd chew him up and spit him out before he knew what happened.

Both women ignored his question.

Kate's grandmother stood with her back rigid. Jared knew Mrs. Evans believed this to be proper posture for a respectable lady. He had to admit it had a certain elegance, but it certainly looked uncomfortable. "A young woman of society does not wait for clothing to wear out. She must set the trends—always be seen wearing the latest styles."

"I'll get Rosalie to sew it up," Kate said. "She doesn't

have fashion sense, but she sets a neat stitch."

"And I'll make sure Rosalie cuts the pattern correctly," his mother-in-law said. "I have pattern books from France."

Jared capitulated. There was little he wouldn't eventually do for his daughter. "I'll give you a note for the store. Charge everything you need."

"You're an angel, Father." Kate entwined her arms around his neck and gave him a quick hug and a kiss on the ear before joining her grandmother at the doorway.

"And buy something for yourself," he told his mother-in-law.

That brought a smile.

"I don't want you seeing a lot of Frank, though," Jared said to Kate's retreating back. "He's not your type. Too quiet, too conservative. There's no fire in him."

He shook his head in wonderment that his daughter could see anything romantic in Frank Larson. "In fact, I'll go with you on Saturday. Tell him we'll meet up with him in town."

Kate made a face, but didn't protest when he invited himself along. "Mr. Larson is refined and learned, Father. He has money and social position."

"Marriage lasts a long time," Jared reminded her. "Marry someone you care deeply about. Don't marry for social position."

It was his maxim.

Kate—the signed mercantile authorization clutched tightly in hand and her petite grandmother in tow—headed toward her bedroom to get dressed for town. She turned at the doorway and said, "You're such an old romantic, Father. We modern women marry for security."

Chapter 11

She'd had it. The burdens of farming were getting to her. Ida's mind felt like it was sloughing through a quagmire and no longer capable of making a decision. Leaving Ernest to fend for himself on the farm after morning chores, she and Peggy took off late Saturday morning on a social trip into Buffalo.

Ida drove the farm wagon with her friend on the seat beside her. They were dressed identically in burgundy dresses of pin-tucked bodices with covered buttons down the front. Ida hadn't felt this good-looking in ages. The quality dress material was purchased with money from last fall's harvest. Peggy spent leisurely winter hours sewing puffed sleeves, dropped waists and full gathered skirts. This was their first chance to show off the garments. They wore wide-brimmed straw bonnets with side slits for the colorful scarves they had tied in bows under their chins. They'd brought woolen shawls in case the weather cooled.

Ida's shotgun was loaded with buckshot and within easy reach under the seat. Peggy had a small pistol in her purse. They would lock both weapons in the wagon's storage box as soon as they arrived at the livery station.

Main Street, where the famous Occidental Hotel was located, was built along what was once a trail that curved down a slight hill, forded Clear Creek, and then angled up the grade on the other side. The town was not named after the animal like anyone would expect, but after Buffalo, New York.

Ida maneuvered the empty wagon down the slight grade of Main Street. She halted at the livery stables, where they made boarding arrangements for the day, then walked back up the hill toward the mercantile store. The Gentrys lived above the store. She was surprised to see the front door wide open and the proprietor standing in the doorway.

"Dearest Ida. We haven't seen you in ages," Herman Gentry said. "And Peggy. Nice to see you again." They were members of the same church which Peggy attended as often as the work on the farm allowed.

He kissed them on the cheek in greeting. "How wonderful you two look. Wait until my Martha finds out you're here."

"What are you doing standing out here, Herman?"

"Special needs of the military. I expect their wagon any time now."

"Maybe I could pick up a few things, too."

"It'd be my pleasure."

Ida brought out her list of specialty items not in her regular supply shipment and arranged for the supplies to be stored in her wagon at the livery stable. Their regular order would be added to the stockpile so the store's wagon wouldn't be needed this week.

"Is Martha home?"

"She's upstairs. Go right up."

Ida and Peggy entered the store and headed for the rear stairs, weaving their way through cramped corridors with countertops and wooden shelving piled dangerously high with any household, farm, ranch or livery items someone living nearby might need. Martha must have heard them coming because she appeared at the top of the narrow stairs before they got one foot on a step.

"Ida," she screamed. "You little devil! Why do you stay away from your friends for so long? And Peggy, too! What a nice surprise." Martha came tripping down the steps to meet Ida and Peggy halfway. They hugged each other enthusiastically, blocking the stairwell, then sorted themselves out with Martha leading the way upstairs.

"To tell the truth," Ida confessed as she climbed the narrow stairs, "I get so tired by day's end that it's all I can do to stay awake to eat, let alone drive to town."

Martha mounted the last of the steps, skirts rustling as she moved, and led them into an elegantly furnished living room. Her gray hair contrasted beautifully with her black taffeta dress. "You work too hard, sweetie. Sell that farm of yours and come live in town."

"She'd never do that, would she?" Peggy was puffing slightly from the climb up the stairs. "The farm keeps her close to Dean."

"You can't hang onto memories forever, dearest. You must start thinking about yourself." Ida knew Martha was a great one for moving on and not looking back.

"I *am* thinking of me. I want to work the farm."

"Well, at least do something that's fun while you're here." Martha ushered them toward two comfortable chairs. "There's a musicale at the church hall tonight. Come with Herman and me."

"Oh, we couldn't," Ida said.

"Yes, you could," Martha insisted. "Stay the night. You two can sleep in our guest room and drive out to the farm after church in the morning."

Ida was tempted, but shook her head.

"It'll do you both good to have a full day off," Martha said.

"We can't," Ida said. "If we don't show up as planned, Ernest will worry. We've been having trouble at the farm lately."

"I've heard rumors." Martha settled herself on the davenport. "Tell me all."

Ida brought her up to date and added, "Art's nephew claims he wants to buy the farm to add on to his uncle's ranch."

Peggy snorted. "Since when did that bunch want more work?"

"They don't take care of what they have," Ida said.

"Isn't that the truth. If he bought, he'd be next door neighbor to Jared Buell. Then he'd better mind his p's and q's. That man won't put up with shenanigans."

"I won't sell, especially to a Campbell."

Martha perched herself on the edge of the davenport's seat. "Beau Campbell's been swaggering around town, making himself obliging to the ladies. Some nitwits are flattered, but he reminds me of a lying snake-oil salesman."

Ida was pleased. She and her long-time friend had come to the same conclusion. "That's exactly my first thought when I laid eyes on him."

"Take your mind off that man," Martha insisted as she settled back against the cushions. "I'd just made coffee and a light snack when you two showed up. Want to join me?"

"It would be a blessing, wouldn't it?" Peggy replied. "It's a pleasure for me to eat someone else's baking."

Martha went to the mahogany sideboard on the far wall of the living room and brought back a large silver tray holding a silver coffee pot with steam coming out of its spout, cream and sugar, a bowl of walnuts, and a small plate of bread cut in squares and buttered.

The aroma of coffee and freshly baked bread filled the air as Martha brought the tray closer and rested it on a nearby rosewood table. Martha distributed lace napkins, delicate china cups and saucers, and silver spoons. Ida couldn't remember the last time she'd had a lace napkin on her lap.

Martha poured.

They'd chatted for what seemed hours when she again urged them to stay over and sleep in the guest room. "At least for one night. Be our guests."

"I wouldn't mind staying over to get caught up with town gossip," Peggy said wistfully.

"A musicale would be nice." A brief touch with civilized behavior would go a long way to counteract Campbell's underhandedness, Ida decided. Burdens were lifting. Someone else would take care of her tonight. Someone else would do the chores tomorrow. Still, she needed someone else's approval to lift the guilt of not doing her share. "What do you say, Peggy?"

"I say we stay."

Martha clapped her hands, a broad smile on her face. "Don't worry about a thing, sweeties. I'll send our delivery boy to the farm to let Ernest know you'll return after church tomorrow."

Ida's heart dropped when she remembered an unfinished chore. "What about our supplies? I asked Herman to store everything I bought in our wagon in the livery stable. The rats will get at them overnight."

"The boy can drive our wagon and deliver the supplies, can't he?" Peggy said.

She should've thought of that herself. She must be tired. "He can stay overnight in our bunkhouse and bring back the wagon in the morning. That'll save us a night's stable fees."

"All settled then, my dears."

The women started tidying up. They stacked the dirty dishes on the sideboard before transporting them to the kitchen, which—to reduce the risk of fire—was on the ground floor in a small building separated from the store by a walkway.

"You two need a chance to rest before the performance." Martha hustled them toward the guest bedroom. "I'll let Herman know we're having overnight company." Martha disappeared into the stairwell to descend to the store. "I need to make arrangements with the delivery boy."

Ida and Peggy settled into the Victorian-furnished guest bedroom. They removed their hats and dresses and hung them on the rack of wall hooks to the left of the bed. Ida poured tepid water into the curved-lip ceramic basin from the large-mouthed pitcher on the mahogany wash stand. Peggy found some monogrammed washcloths and towels stacked in the cabinet underneath its marble top. They washed off road dust before pulling the heavy, deep purple curtains closed against the brilliance of the sun to darken the room for a nap.

Martha had a good idea in convincing them to stay over and get a break from the farm. It was the first time in ages that she could nap in the afternoon and attend a social occasion in the evening.

When they returned to the parlor after a nap and a sponge bath, Martha told them "Believe me, the dear boy is excited. It's not often he gets to sleep away from home."

In what seemed like no time at all to Ida, she and Peggy had been exquisitely fed in the Occidental dining room and were in the church social hall. As she was sitting down, her breath caught in her throat. Seated in the front row with his daughter and mother-in-law was Jared Buell. He was talking quietly with a man sitting at his daughter's side. Ida recognized the small man as the banker, Frank Larson. He was in his early thirties. His high forehead was perpetually creased in thought and he was always nattily dressed. He moved with quick, jerky movements that reminded Ida of a chipmunk constantly in motion.

She flushed, afraid that her face would be beet red by the time her rear reached the hard, wooden seat. In the past, meeting up with her neighbor would've been easy—they would've cordially ignored each other. But how could she now? He'd helped her fight the fire. He'd had coffee in her kitchen. He'd saved her wagon from tipping over. He'd...

She slouched down, trying to make her large frame invisible.

She was remembering one thing she learned during the fire: he looked good without his shirt on.

Hadn't been able to forget that.

* * * *

Jared heard his daughter hiss to his mother-in-law. "There's that hulking neighbor of ours. And she's wearing red. She looks bigger than ever."

As surreptitiously as possible—considering his head stuck above most of the other heads in the audience—he twisted in his seat to find Ida. She was about seven rows back. He scowled. What was she doing scrunching down in her seat like that?

Unladylike or not, something about her drew him. Opposite his daughter's opinion, Jared thought the burgundy color nicely offset Ida's sun-darkened skin. A warm spot of admiration grew near his heart. Her abundant dark hair was not braided, but caught up on top of her head with sparkling combs. Probably Martha Gentry's doing, he thought when he saw his friend sitting close to Ida. He was pleased she'd convinced his neighbor to look less like a farmer and more like a woman tonight. Although most of the hair was held in place by combs, a few strands escaped and lay tauntingly against flushed cheeks. His fingers itched to tuck them back in place.

Ida looked up—her cornflower blue eyes clear and bright—her wide mouth tempting. Her steady gaze made him embarrassed for gawking. He nodded a cool greeting and turned back in his seat to concentrate on what his daughter was saying.

* * * *

Ida drew herself upright, her head held high, her shoulders thrown back. She'd enjoy the music and ignore her aloof neighbor. No use trying to be invisible. The reason for invisibility already knew she was in this very seat in the church hall.

Just because she'd had some passing interest in Jared Buell didn't mean she needed to alter her life to include him. She was getting along just fine on her own. Certainly, she'd seen some admirable qualities in him, qualities that she hadn't noticed in the past—probably, for the reason that the only man to hold her attention was Dean. Besides, it wasn't as if he'd had a great change of heart toward her. After all, he didn't look that excited to see her when she'd caught his eye a minute ago.

Laughter burst from the back of the hall. A cold chill swept across her shoulders. She recognized one of the voices. Surreptitiously, she turned to look. Beau Campbell stepped through the doorway, talking animatedly with two town men as if they were his great friends.

Ida turned back, again wishing for invisibility. Her neighbor's distinctive footsteps came inexorably closer as he and the men made their way down the aisle, stopping often to chat.

She was surprised at how many people Campbell knew. It hadn't been that long that he'd been in the neighborhood. He must've made a point of introducing himself around town. It wasn't like he'd built up friendships in the past by being a frequent visitor at his uncle's ranch. As far as Ida knew, this was his first visit. She wondered if these good citizens knew how he was harassing her.

A shiver ran along her spine. Her disappointment ran deep. She'd come to town to get away from trouble and here it was walking in her direction. She dreaded what Campbell would do when he recognized her.

I might need a strong ally like Jared Buell after all, she thought.

Ida pasted a smile on her face and wondered if she should let Peggy know that Beau was in the room. Perhaps it was best to allow her friend to remain oblivious and in animated conversation with Martha.

She watched as Jared turned slightly in his chair and caught a glimpse of Campbell. His shoulders stiffened. At the same time, Ida heard a slight hesitation to Beau's step before he told the two men that he was going to sit in the back with friends.

Reprieve.

She heard the scraping of a chair as he sat. By the sounds of their voices, he was enthusiastically greeting two women.

Jared slightly raised a questioning eyebrow as if to ask if she was all right with Campbell in the hall. She nodded. She was all right for at least as long as she and Peggy stayed out of arm's length of that hateful man.

The lights dimmed and the music started. She did her best to drive the image of Beau out of her head and concentrate on the performance. She did her best not worry about how she would handle the intermission.

* * * *

During the twenty minutes break for intermission while she and Peggy had their heads together, deciding what to do, Jared had come up behind her in the aisle. He touched her lightly on the waist to catch her attention. His daughter and mother-in-law, with the banker in tow, brushed past their grouping without acknowledgment. The first words out of Jared's mouth were, "Beau Campbell's at the back of the social hall."

"Wouldn't you think we'd be given at least this one break from that man?" Peggy said.

"Look," Martha said. "There he goes."

"Where?" Peggy asked.

"He's going out the door with Miss Dawson and her mother on either arm."

Ida felt relief.

"He'll be too occupied to bother us," Peggy said. Ida hoped she was right.

"Shall I walk out with you?" Jared asked.

"Please do," Martha Gentry said, taking her husband's arm and turning towards the door.

"What about your daughter?" Ida asked. "Don't you need to stay with her?" She didn't verbalize the thought that the daughter wouldn't want to join any grouping with Ida in its midst.

"Mr. Larson claimed her and her grandmother for the intermission."

"Oh, well then…," she said.

Jared took Ida's and Peggy's arms and walked them out into the lantern-lit night. He steered them to an isolated corner of the church lawn. Martha and Herman followed.

"Wouldn't you know it." Martha sounded annoyed. "They're going to the refreshments table. It'll be awkward getting punch."

Ida turned her back so she could no longer see Beau. "I don't care. I'll do without."

"Me, too," Peggy said, although she didn't look happy.

The sky was dark with a new moon. Kerosene lanterns were strategically placed about the refreshments table and the graveled walkways. Tree toads and crickets mingled tones with the animated voices of the concert goers. If it weren't for the presence of her outlaw neighbor, Ida would've found this a pleasant night indeed.

"That's a beautiful dress you're wearing," Jared said. "The style and the color suit you."

Ida looked down at the glossy material, catching the light from the lanterns, to hide a blush. It had been years since she'd had a compliment on her looks.

"I made these," Peggy said. "The pattern is complicated."

"She's very talented," Ida said.

"Are you enjoying the musicale, Mr. Buell?" Peggy asked.

He nodded. "I decided at the last minute to accompany my daughter and her grandmother."

"Isn't that your daughter talking with Miss Dawson and the others?" Herman Gentry asked. "I thought you said she was staying away from Campbell."

Ida heard Jared's sharp intake of breath and a muffled "Damn."

"Excuse me," he said with a slight, stiff bow. Dropping her hand from his arm, he strode toward the refreshments table.

The bell sounded the return to seats. Herman Gentry urged them inside, but Ida dawdled and saw Campbell and the two women leave the refreshments table before Jared caught up to his daughter and mother-in-law.

* * * *

Jared was steaming. Only days ago, his daughter had said she'd have nothing to do with Beau Campbell. Yet, less than two minutes ago, she was in cordial conversation with the man. He glared at his mother-in-law. She should've stopped it. "Didn't I tell you to have nothing to do with that man?"

Kate drew herself upright and took in a deep breath through her nose, her chin up. She looked anything but contrite. "I couldn't be ungracious to my dear friend and her mother. I said as little as possible."

Even without a confirming Pinkerton report, Jared had become convinced Beau was his old enemy, especially with his cattle being rustled. He feared for his daughter. He hadn't been there to protect his brother and sister-in-law from this man, but, by God, he'd protect his daughter. "He's a snake. He'll find a way into your company and stab you in the back if you give him the slightest opportunity."

"Surely you're wrong," Larson said. "He's become a big depositor."

"Probably on stolen money." Jared had forgotten about Frank Larson. He should have been more circumspect with a guest looking on. Too late now.

"Mon père, I'm no longer a child. I can make my own decisions."

Jared grabbed her arm and pulled her toward him. "Listen to me, girl, you're not as grown up as you think if you associate with the likes of that man."

Kate looked humiliated and near tears.

"Leave it be, Jared." His mother-in-law slapped at his hand with her fan. "I was with her all the time. This is a church function. What could happen?"

Jared struggled to calm down. A split in the family with Beau getting on Kate's good side could be disastrous— something he couldn't afford.

"Indeed, Mr. Buell," Larson said. "I'm watching out for your daughter's interests."

That statement hardly comforted Jared.

"Don't create a spectacle." Mrs. Evans spoke in a stern tone. "The gong has rung. We need to return to our seats."

He looked around and saw people looking their way. He decided to let the matter rest for now.

"We'll talk about this back at the hotel tonight," he said through gritted teeth.

Jared reached for his daughter's arm to walk her back inside, but Kate jerked her arm away.

"If you're going to be evil, I don't want to sit near you. Come, Grandmamma, Mr. Larson. We'll find other seats and find our own way back to the hotel."

"You'll do nothing of the kind," Jared said, but Kate had grabbed her grandmother's arm and was already catching up with the crowd returning to the hall. Frank Larson trailed behind.

Jared stood, fuming, crickets and tree toads making a racket around him. Mingled with his fury was an element of defeat. That confrontation with his daughter hadn't gone well. He turned sharply on his heel and headed back inside, conscious of the furtive glances his way. He hunched his shoulders as if that would protect him.

Beau's expression was smug when Jared walked alone down the aisle to his original seat. That smugness seared into Jared's gut.

* * * *

Later that night, Beau Campbell and his uncle were in the nearly empty barroom of a saloon off Main Street. Agitated, he paced the rough-boarded floor. Diablo sprawled across a nearby chair. "That woman should've tucked her tail under her legs and run."

His uncle clucked his tongue. "Always been tough. Should've seen her getting' the sheriff riled up agin' me when her man git kilt."

"Well, you deliberately shot him."

"Never proved it."

Beau stopped pacing and faced his uncle. "What can I do to break that insufferable female?"

Art spit tobacco towards the corner of the room, completely missing the spittoon. "Attack 'er through 'er soft heart."

"What do you mean?"

"She can't stand seein' people hurt. Shoot that boy she hired."

"Kill the boy?"

"Fer God's sake, no." Art's face got red with irritation.

"We'd 'ave the whole a Johnson County down upon us."

"Well, what then?"

"Wing 'im."

"I'll do it," Diablo spoke as he chewed on a piece of jerky.

"They'll get suspicious if they see you," he told Diablo.

"A stray bullet while hunting," Art said. "It'll look like an accident. I'll even pay for the doctorin'."

Beau tumbled the idea around and liked it. He ordered his uncle and Diablo home with the name of the man to do the job. He needed to stay visible in town. He needed an alibi.

Chapter 12

The next morning, Ida looked for Jared as she walked to Sunday services with Peggy and the Gentrys. She told herself she wasn't disappointed when he was nowhere to be seen.

Probably everyone last night was aware that Miss Buell, her grandmother and Mr. Larson sat on the left side of the social hall when they returned from intermission. Not that it was her business, but Ida was curious to know what had been said.

The First United Methodist Church welcomed her with its double doors flung open. Arched, stained glass windows, encased in white framing, topped the doorway, with black metal railings edging the two wide steps leading up to the white clapboard church.

Peals of laughter rang out from energetic children who raced in madcap circles, chasing each other in a game of tag. They looked like they were taking full advantage of final moments of play before being forced to sit quietly with folded hands for the morning's Sunday School Bible lesson.

Herman Gentry led the way through the vestibule and

into the high-ceiling sanctuary where many worshippers already congregated. Ida didn't hold back a small smile when she discovered that Jared was one of the worshippers. He sat in a front pew, with his daughter next to him and Mr. Larson and his mother-in-law to the far side. The Gentrys chose a pew a couple of rows to the rear. From the set of Kate Buell's shoulders, she could tell the girl was still angry.

Ida looked, but didn't see Beau Campbell anywhere. Relieved, she settled herself as comfortably as possible on the wooden pew. Sunlight entered the sanctuary through tall, slender windows arched at the top. On the rear wall, high above the altar, a round, stained glass window featuring a white dove with an olive branch in its beak filtered sunbeams onto an intricately carved wooden pulpit.

The choir entered the sanctuary through an interior door while singing "Rock of Ages." The congregation rose and joined in. Jared's baritone drifted back to where she held the corner of the hymnal shared with Peggy. Ida followed the lyrics with her eyes until she picked up at the chorus, adding her alto to the blend. She rose and sat with the others, even while her mind wasn't focused on the service. The soothingly familiar music made her want to drift off and catch up on the sleep she'd missed last night when she tossed and turned, unable to get her two un-alike neighbors out of her mind. One neighbor she wanted totally out of her life and the other was increasingly moving in.

Fortunately, the minister wasn't long-winded. Soon the service was over and the pastor and the choir were passing down the center aisle. The congregants rose to follow. Without seeing it happen, she knew when Jared came up behind her. He touched her arm and she tried not to look too eager as she turned toward him. "Good morning."

She wished she wasn't wearing the same dress as yesterday. Kate and her grandmother outshone her with their freshly ironed frocks. She self-consciously touched her hair to make sure that at least her braid was securely in place and presentable.

Jared included Frank Larson, his daughter and mother-in-law in the introduction. Ida could hear the coolness in Kate's greeting. They moved slowly down the aisle with the rest of the congregants, while Mr. Larson stayed close and attentive to Miss Buell. After saying farewells to the pastor and his wife, they chatted quietly on the sidewalk in front of the church.

"May I invite all of you to join us as my guests for a meal at the Occidental?" Jared asked after a while. "We plan to dine before going home."

"Delighted." Martha Gentry spoke before Ida was able to remind her friend she'd sent word to Ernest that they'd return right after church.

"Well, I don't know..." Ida started to say.

"How kind," Peggy said, excitedly. "Isn't it the truth that I hardly ever get to eat someone else's cooking?"

Ida shot her a look that said *"we should get back to the farm"*—which her friend ignored.

"But Ernest expects..."

"It'll give us time for a long chat." Martha cut Ida off and wrapped her arm through that of her husband. They started toward the hotel after he had offered his other arm to Peggy.

"Dining in the company of charming ladies will be my great pleasure," the banker said to the women in general, but he was looking longingly at Kate. He offered his support to Miss Buell and her grandmother.

It seemed to Ida like she was odd man out. She might as well capitulate, even though she didn't think that being at table with Jared's daughter and mother-in-law would aid in keeping food down.

Ida was left standing on the sidewalk until Jared came alongside and placed her hand upon his forearm. When she glanced up, she caught the ghost of a smile on his usually serious face.

* * * *

The Occidental Hotel dining room was crowded when they arrived. To Ida's relief, their party separated among several small tables, each tastefully set. The banker—greeted heartedly by the proprietor—was led to a prime location near the window with Miss Buell and her grandmother. Peggy was seated with the Gentrys near the entrance. Ida found herself alone at a table with Jared, tucked in a corner near the kitchen.

"I hope you don't mind being away from your friend," he was saying. "My daughter wanted to talk with Mr. Larson. For those conversations, a grandmother is a more tolerant chaperone. Besides, she's angry with me and wouldn't make an easy table companion."

"Quite all right," Ida said.

"Not the most desirable of tables," he said as he looked around at the crowded tables, "but it's the last one to be had. We'd have a long wait to get a better one."

"I'm not picky," she said. "Besides, I should get back to the farm so Ernest doesn't worry. There have been too many close calls of late."

"We'll ride out with you so you and Peggy will be safe. No one will challenge a large group."

A warm glow built near her heart at the offer.

He picked up the menu. "What would you like?"

She looked over the selection and chose lamb grown locally in the nearby town of Kaycee. Her sheep were for wool, not eating. It would be a treat to eat lamb, especially because the hotel chef was renowned for it.

They ordered and were settling into polite conversation when a voice that brought a chill to her backbone spoke loudly from a distance behind her right shoulder.

"Why, Miz Osterbach, fancy meeting you in this vulnerable establishment."

Beau Campbell. A shiver traveled down Ida's spine.

"This is a most fortunate of opportunities." She heard him stroll closer.

"Mr. Campbell," Ida said, refusing to look at him. "I don't wish to be rude, but your company is not wanted."

"Now, now," Beau said, ignoring her snub. "Let's not let some little disagreements cause a strain between us. We may yet come to an understanding."

"No, we won't," Ida said.

Jared rose, his hands at his sides curved into fists. He cleared his throat which drew Beau's attention to him. "The lady doesn't wish to speak with you."

Ida realized she hadn't introduced the two men. Jared should know with whom he was dealing. "Forgive me," she said to Jared. "You may not know who this is. Mr. Buell, may I introduce Mr. Beaufort Campbell, nephew to Art Campbell." She reluctantly turned to Beau. "This is Mr. Jared Buell, my neighbor on the other side."

"Beau to my friends," he said ingratiatingly as he gave a slight bow. She thought his face seemed redder than when he first arrived in the dining room.

Jared wasn't mollified and forced words between gritted teeth. "I repeat, the lady doesn't want your company." The rancher held his ground, giving evidence that he would fight if it came down to that.

"I see this is not the importune moment to press my interests." Beau stepped back and looked around the room. "No more tables. I'll go across the street. The food's better."

She saw that he put his hat back on while still indoors. *Not the gentleman he pretends to be,* she decided.

Ida expelled the deep breath she was holding, ignoring that the sound was unladylike. "I let that man get under my skin," she confessed when Jared sat back down. "Like a bad rash."

* * * *

"I wish..." Kate said whimsically a few minutes after Beau Campbell had showed up at her father's table in the restaurant. She deliberately let the unexplained wish hang in the air and allowed her gaze longingly to meet with Frank Larson's across the Occidental's elegantly set table. She wore a yellow outfit with tiny white rosebuds and a high collar with a significant plunge that she knew tantalizingly accentuated her slender neck and dark hair. She leaned toward the banker. She wanted to entice him into accommodating her wish without her father knowing. Kate's grandmother looked on indulgently.

"Any wish by a charming girl like you should be fulfilled." Frank Larson smiled benevolently. "What is it?"

"I wish I could find some way to make life difficult for that woman talking with my father. He pays too much attention to her and she's not at our social level."

"Kate, dear," her grandmother said as she lay down her soup spoon. The hovering waiter immediately whisked away the empty soup bowl. "That's unkind. What will Mr. Larson think?"

The banker turned to Mrs. Evans. "I realize, dear lady, that there are people with whom we would prefer not to associate."

"We can hardly state it in public." Mrs. Evans' tone was disapproving.

"Look," Kate hissed, "that Mr. Campbell is talking with father. Last night Papa yelled at me for just that."

"The conversation doesn't look pleasant," Frank Larson said. "I do hope your father doesn't upset the man."

"Mr. Campbell is very rough around the edges," her grandmother said with a censoring frown. "Like your father, I didn't approve of last night's episode, but I approved less of his making a scene."

"Mr. Campbell's been transferring considerable funds into our bank." Larson sounded anxious. "Your father's not involved with day-to-day transactions. He may upset the apple cart with a wrong word."

"Poor Mr. Campbell. He looks so embarrassed," Kate said.

"I do hope your father doesn't upset a big depositor." Larson looked like he was considering bounding up from his seat and racing across the room to smooth out any problems.

"Look! Mr. Campbell's going away and that woman's looking upset." Kate's chin rose in self justification. "I'd like her worse than upset. I'd like her in real trouble."

"Kathryn!" Mrs. Evans looked scandalized.

"Well, something to keep her occupied and so she stays away from Father," Kate said. "I don't like women finagling their way into my mother's spot."

"Not every woman is out to marry your father," her grandmother admonished. "I doubt she's interested. I'm told she was deeply in love with her late husband."

"I don't care," Kate said, a pout appearing. "See the way Father is looking at her. You'd think he wanted to be her white knight."

"I see no such thing," her grandmother said. "That's all in your imagination, my dear."

"She probably egged him on to chase Mr. Campbell away." Kate refused to be diverted from her beliefs.

"She's a customer of our bank," Frank Larson said. "That's probably why your father is paying attention to her."

"She's a customer?"

"Has been for years. I hold the mortgage on the farm."

Kate flashed a brilliant smile. "Good. Call it and chase her out when she's not able to pay."

Her grandmother gasped. "A lady doesn't interfere in the business of gentlemen."

The banker looked horrified and Kate decided she'd stepped over the line. She back-pedaled. She could afford to bide her time. After all, Larson was potential husband material. She didn't want to destroy that bond because of a fit of ire. Kate patted the banker's sleeve and sighed. "I know you can't do anything like that. It just wouldn't do."

She allowed her hand to linger under her grandmother's watchful eye. "I was letting out my frustration."

"Unbecoming, my dear," her grandmother admonished.

Kate smiled wanly, her drama coaching at finishing school coming in handy. "I'd feel so much better if I knew she was occupied with something other than my father."

"There is a small seed loan," Larson said slowly. "That would be easier to call. I wouldn't have to explain my action to the board."

"Good. Call that."

"Kate, dear," Mrs. Evans said, drawing herself upright with a stern expression on her face. "This is most unseemly. A lady is not aggressive. She nurtures and heals."

Kate tried to look humble and repentant. "Grandmama is right, of course. This is all wishful thinking."

She saw a determined expression cross Larson's face. She'd laid the seed. She wondered if it would grow.

"Our meal is here," her grandmother said when the waiter arrived at their table carrying dishes on a large tray. "Let's not spoil it with such talk. Speak on more pleasant topics."

* * * *

Disgruntled, Beau slunk out of the Occidental with no meal in his belly. Despite his boast of eating at the hotel restaurant across the street, he couldn't take the chance of hanging around town and possibly inviting another altercation. He didn't need closer scrutiny from Buell.

He cursed the farmer woman. She was so big she'd blocked his view from the restaurant doorway. The tucked-away angle of the table could have proved a setup for disaster. He hadn't realized there was a man with her and that that man was Jared Buell until he'd already spoken— irretrievably alerting them to his approach. Anger had infused him as he recognized the trap he'd unwittingly entered.

But Lady Luck stuck with him. Buell hadn't recognized him, even after that unfortunate introduction. All Jared did was stand up and warn him off on behalf of that female. There was no sign of recognition in his voice or in his words.

Beau had been pointedly staying out of the rancher's way until he could arrange a time where he'd have an opportunity to shoot him in apparent self-defense. He certainly hadn't planned on this spontaneous meeting.

Red hot anger rose from the pit of his stomach to lodge in his throat as he remembered his humiliation. The woman had the gall to cold shoulder him in a roomful of important diners. He'd have a hard time explaining the snub away the next time he went to town.

* * * *

Ida's appetite had disappeared with the appearance of Beau Campbell. With the distress she was feeling, her stomach couldn't do justice to her meal. She would've asked the kitchen help to wrap the delicacy to take home, except that she didn't want to look like a pauper who saved scraps of food.

After the waiter departed with the dirty dishes and the coffee was served, she and Jared talked about her troubles with Campbell and what to do. By the time the others finished their desserts, Ida felt she'd forged a strong alliance with this rancher.

* * * *

No sooner had Ida arrived at home on Sunday afternoon from her overnight stay with the Gentrys when she took off again, riding an exhausted Molly to the Bar J ranch. She dismounted at the ranch's kitchen door and rushed in to talk with Sadie Mason, who was washing dishes.

"I'm told Todd was shot." She could hear the unease in her voice.

"That's right." Sadie leisurely dried her hands. "But he's fine. One of Campbell's wranglers was out shootin' partridges and hit Todd by chance."

"I doubt that crowd does anything by chance."

"The pellets just grazed my boy's arm." Sadie hung the towel. "Rosalie patched him up."

Relief swept through Ida that the boy was not seriously injured. Jared had the right of it. Todd's hiring was more dangerous than she knew. The boy got injured because of her ignorance.

"The ranch hand came here to apologize," Sadie said. "If it were deliberate, I don't see why he'd come."

"There's always an underhanded reason," Ida said grimly.

"Ruined my boy's good shirt, it did. I was thinking of askin' for a new shirt, but I didn't."

"You should have."

Sadie offered her a seat, but Ida was too upset to sit. She rocked from foot-to-foot where she stood. "Did any pellets hit bone?"

Sadie shook her head. "Barely bled."

"That's a blessing."

"Art Campbell came. Said he'd pick up the doctoring expenses, but we didn't have any."

Ida grimaced. "They're putting on a show."

"Todd won't be riding for a few days."

"I think it's become too dangerous for him. He can help with the harvest where the men are around, but he shouldn't be out on his own."

Sadie shook her head. "That'll upset my Todd. He's real proud of his work."

Ida left for the bedroom to check on the boy. She decided to wait until he was completely healed before she told him he was out of a job.

"Shucks, Miz Osterbach. It ain't nothin'." He showed his patched arm. "It's not even my best arm."

"What were you doing in the fields on a Sabbath?" she asked.

"I was afeared someone might drag another dead deer to the water. I was checkin' the creek. Jumping Jehosaphat, it ain't like I had somethin' else to do."

"But you got shot for your troubles."

"Not deliberate like."

"It could very well have been deliberate."

After more assurances from Todd that he was fine, she left the bedroom and returned to the kitchen to find Jared sitting at the table drinking a mug of coffee.

"I came to see about Todd," he said.

"I was just with him." Ida shook her head in bewilderment. "He seems to be proud of having been shot."

Jared grinned. "Young boys are like that."

"It scares me," Ida said. "They did this while we were both away."

"It disturbs me. He's my tenant."

"Let it be, Mr. Buell." Sadie put a mug of coffee in front of Ida. "It's settled."

"Sticks in my craw," Jared said.

"I didn't tell Todd, but I'm stopping his job. You were right and I was wrong. It's too dangerous."

"My son can handle himself," Sadie said. "He got himself right back here to be patched up as soon as it happened. Didn't make a sound while Rosalie worked on him."

"I'll think about it," Ida said.

While she sat in the warm kitchen at the oil-cloth covered table, the bitterness of the coffee matched her mood. She left the ranch with a lot on her mind.

Chapter 13

"It's going to be a good year," Ida decided as she arched her back and stretched her arms high in the air. She shook out her tired shoulders, then put her hands on her hips while she looked out over her land.

It was Friday, a week after her visit with the Gentrys. She'd just finished planting the seed potatoes from last year's crop preserved for this year's growing stock. The carrots, squash and string beans were planted and the weather was cooperating.

After ten years, the land had finally become productive, well above its original marginal condition. For years she and Dean struggled to work manure and compost into these acres near the farmhouse kept fenced against wild animals. It was finally paying off.

Last night, she'd taken care of her accounts. Financially, she was holding her own. If things kept going this well for the next four months—and if she had as good a crop as she expected—she'd have extra money above her mortgage and loan payments to improve the property. Ida allowed herself the satisfaction of a job well done.

She and Dean had staked out this land and protected it from unscrupulous homesteaders and marauders. Old Molly, always dependable, had strained to drag an iron blade under the matted roots of the grasses, with Dean using every ounce of strength to keep the plow angled in the right direction. He broke the hard soil, while she took out the rocks. They sweated over the ground that sustained their married life.

With Dean gone, this land was all she had to make her life worthwhile. She'd fight tooth and nail to protect it.

Chapter 14

That evening, Jared stepped onto his front porch, took a deep breath of fresh air and leaned against a Doric style post. Eyes closed, he listened to the night sounds of insects and animals.

The ranch buildings benefited from the shade of the cottonwoods and the willows growing near the banks of Clear Creek, yet the buildings were still positioned well above flood level. Year by year, as needs arose, he'd added structures. Everything had a use and a place in the daily workings of this ranch which he and his men defended against marauding enemies—human or otherwise.

The past weeks Jared had quietly been hiring gunfighters against the inevitable showdown with Campbell. Once he had proof in hand, he'd act. In the meantime, if Beau or his cohorts fired the first shot, they'd learn soon enough that they'd invaded a hornet's nest.

Since talking with Ida Osterbach on Sunday, he'd been thinking a lot about his time spent in Kansas. He no longer felt as guilty as he once did about the decision to move to Wyoming. Isabella had been an integral part in that decision.

She'd been willing to give him time to build a fortune from beef before returning in style to the East Coast. That she'd sickened before it could come about was a tragedy, but not one of his making.

He heard his daughter step out of the house to sit on the porch swing. They'd had an uneasy truce since that night in the church hall. Jared slowly opened his eyes. Pushing away from the post, he walked over to sit next to Kate on the swing. He took her hand in both of his, surprised as always at how fine-boned it was.

"Give up on the card game?" he asked.

"Grandmamma got tired. She's gone to bed early."

"We could have a game."

"Be prepared to lose, mon pére," she teased. "I crush all opponents."

Jared believed it. Despite her delicate features, his daughter had iron in her backbone and a need to bend life to her will.

He decided to share his concerns.

"Dear heart, I don't want you to worry," he said as he stroked her hand, thoughtfully, "but I'm expecting trouble when I prove that Beau Campbell and his roughnecks are behind the cattle rustling."

Put under pressure, Beau's true nature would come out. A fight was inevitable. Jared saw no way that Beau would remain the chivalrous gentleman he was portraying in town.

"*Mon Dieu*, Papa." Concern crossed her face. "Don't do anything foolish."

"I'll talk with the sheriff first if I can," Jared said. "I've already wired both him and the marshal, but Matt's tied up in Cheyenne."

"Too bad. I would've enjoyed seeing Uncle Matt," Kate said, using her childhood title for Jared's friend.

"Hopefully, Sheriff Angus is on his way back." Jared's brows furrowed. "I talked with Deputy Trainer and he doesn't seem to have the backbone for a fight."

"That might be for the best, Papa. After all, Mr. Campbell is making friends in town. It might be best not to rock the boat."

"I can't agree. Bullies have to be stopped. Quickly."

Tension squeezed his chest as he reluctantly revealed his decision. "I don't want you near here if bullets start flying. I'm sending you and your grandmother to Sheridan." Emptiness would fill the ranch house when Kate left, but he'd sacrifice his wellbeing for her safety.

"Really, Father? How wonderful. The shopping is so much better in Sheridan."

"Check with your grandmother and let me know if she'd be ready to travel by next week's end or by the following at the latest."

Kate sprung up from the porch swing and hurried toward the open front door. "I'll see if she's still awake."

"I'll prepare a bank draft for your expenses when I'm in town this week," he said to her disappearing back.

Once again he was alone, with only the night sounds for company.

* * * *

In the Campbell kitchen that next evening, Beau and his uncle were drinking a better brand of whiskey than his uncle's usual rotgut. No one else was around.

"Heard Buell is shippin' that kid of hizen to Sheridan with her gram," Art said. "Stayin' a while, too."

Beau took another swallow and scowled.

"Good riddance to that highfalutin snot. Last Wednesday, she crossed the street rather than say good morning."

His uncle spit toward the spittoon. "Thinks her shit's perfumed."

"Pissed me off."

"But she's not yer problem," his uncle said around a swallow. "Her pa is."

"He's runnin' scared. That's why he's shipping her out."

"Maybe. Maybe not."

Beau looked at his uncle. "Why else?"

"Could be settin' up for a fight. Wants 'er out the way."

"Fight or run makes no difference. I can handle that son of a bitch."

His uncle looked at him over the top of the whiskey bottle. "Some say he's tagged you with that Kansas bank killin'."

Beau sneered. "Took him long enough to figure that one out."

"Watch yerself, my boy. Some say he wired the Pinkertons. Wants to see if there's a warrant out, don't he?"

"So what? They can't prove nothing. It was too long ago."

His uncle took a swig, swished it around and swallowed. "He's out to git you."

"Good excuse to kill the bastard." Beau amended his

statement. "In self-defense, of course."

They both smirked.

* * * *

Mouth agape, Ida stared at the official bank document that had arrived on the store's wagon with the weekly delivery. The legal language swam before her eyes. It explained how the bank had a right to get its money back just by asking for it—and it was asking for the crop money back before the harvest was in. Her stomach churned when she read that the deadline for payment was one month from yesterday. When the full impact of the bank's request hit her, the envelope fell to the floor and she slumped into a kitchen chair.

"What is it?" Peggy laid a hand on Ida's shoulder in a calming gesture.

"The bank." Ida's voice sounded strained. "They want the crop loan back. They only give me until next month."

"Let me see that." Peggy snatched the bank's letter out of Ida's hands and swooped down to catch up its envelope from the floor. She pulled out a kitchen chair, plunked herself into it and spread the official-looking letter out flat on the kitchen table. She squinted as she read.

"They sure take a lot of words to say something, don't they?" Peggy looked up at Ida. "What brought this on, do you think?"

Ida shrugged her shoulders. "This is the first time our crop loan's been called early."

"It can't be nothing you did," Peggy said. "All your payments are on time, aren't they?"

"I wonder how many other farmers have been hit with recalls," Ida said, half to herself. She could scrape together the money, but it would leave them tight until the harvest. She swallowed hard. The call was a major disruption to her well-planned finances.

"You need to talk with Frank Larson," Peggy said. "He's the one who sent this."

"He never even gave us a hint of this call when we saw him at the musicale two weeks ago." If this was new bank policy, she'd have to find another way to finance next year's planting. Maybe the Gentrys. "This means," Ida said, "the money won't be there for lumber to rebuild the burned-out shed."

"It's a crime, that's what it is," Peggy said. "Puts us to extra trouble."

No winter hay shed meant the men would be lugging bales from the barn to the cattle in the fields.

"Wait until Ernest hears," Peggy said. "He'll be spitting fire."

Ida shook her head, bewildered. "I've got to get to the bottom of this. I'll go into town next week."

Chapter 15

Ten days of unremitting sunshine melted the mountain snow. Alarmed, Ida recognized that Clear Creek was rising faster than its usual spring swelling. The rushing waters were pushing small stones along the creek bottom with relentless force. This year it was as if the waters were in an extra hurry. The rushing sound was no longer the resonance of nourishing waters for crops. These waters menaced. She really didn't need another problem on top of the crop loan call.

Her cousin was about a hundred feet away, walking the rows of crops to check their growth. Ida called to him.

"Ernest."

She waved her arms in wide arcs to catch his attention in case her voice didn't carry over the noise of the water. "Come here and take a look at the creek. I think it's too high for this time of year."

Ernest trotted to her side. His plaid flannel shirt, necessary in the cool of early morning, was unbuttoned now to counteract the sun's warmth which beat down from a cloudless sky. His large frame reminded her of her brother's. The brown corduroy trousers weren't muddy like usual. With the crops planted, their daily chores now mostly kept them on their feet or bending over, not grubbing in the ground.

"What are you doing out here?" Ernest asked when he came close. "I thought you were taking this Friday off. I thought you needed a rest to get over what the bank's doing to you."

It was true that she wore a small-print, flowered dress with ruffles at the end of tapered sleeves and a full bib apron to protect it. A wide-brimmed straw bonnet was tied securely under her chin. She'd given herself the treat of free time to stroll about and savor the anticipation of this year's crop. If Jared Buell came pleasantly to mind as she walked along, so be it. It kept the image of Frank Larson at bay.

"I decided on a walk. This is as far as I got."

"Well, don't tire yourself."

"The creek's worrying me." She pointed out how close the water was to the high-water mark on the side of the embankment.

"I'll check it out towards the Bar J," he said as he as he walked away. "You check in the other direction and I'll meet you back here."

Ida was thankful that Ernest willingly tackled whatever task came to hand, never shirking responsibility. If the water kept rising, she wouldn't go to town tomorrow to talk with Larson. The bank loan could wait a couple of weeks. The water level of the creek would not.

She walked the creek in the direction which would take her toward the road to the Campbell ranch. As she walked she became more troubled. The part of the stream she first looked at was not an aberration. Sections of the creek bed and banks were already being gouged out by the rapidly moving water. *Not good,* she thought. If they got a spring thunderstorm on top of this, they'd be in trouble.

She'd seen enough. Ida turned back and waited for Ernest under a tall willow tree. She removed her plaid apron to sit on it and lean back against the tree trunk. She closed her eyes to focus on what to do to protect her farm. A short time later, she was startled by Ernest who was slumping down beside her against the willow trunk. He'd taken off his hat and was shaking his head, looking solemn.

"That creek's building up for trouble."

"It's already taking parts of the embankment down stream," she said, "and it's not even at flood stage."

"The men and I can spend today and tomorrow shoring up the banks."

Unless there was an emergency, they'd normally take the Sabbath off. This week was the exception.

"I can help." Ida scrambled to her feet. "Let me get out of these clothes."

Ernest grabbed her shoulders and pushed her back down. "Stay put. Today's your day off. Give yourself a break for once."

"But—" Ida started to say. Ernest put a hand lightly over her mouth.

"No buts. Give us credit for being able to tackle things without you telling us how."

Ida was stunned. She didn't consider herself bossy. "I don't mean...to suggest...you can't handle...the shoring up...yourself," she stammered.

"I know you don't mean to, but you do. This once, let me do things my way." He rose to his feet and started walking away.

"Sure," Ida said in almost a whisper. Then she leaned back against the tree trunk, pretending she could rest when her farm was in danger.

As soon as Ernest was out of sight, she scurried toward the farmhouse. She decided that—while the men filled dozens of potato sacks with farmland rocks kept for such emergencies—she'd drive the wagon to the Bar J for help. Jared could divert water from his stretch of creek out over his meadowlands. That way less water would carry through onto her crops.

Ida stayed in her dress, but removed the bibbed apron and changed her heavy work boots for soft leather ones. While she changed her shoes, her heart pounded at the prospect of seeing her neighbor. She hadn't seen him since their Sunday meal at the Occidental.

* * * *

Upon arriving at the Bar J mid-afternoon, the excited bustle of activity at the ranch house caught Ida by surprise. Jared's daughter and mother-in-law sat on colorful cushions in a surrey with a fringed sun cover. Ida caught the ugly look Kate sent her way.

Slightly behind the surrey was a wagon hitched to a substantial ox. The wagoner waited patiently, his hand on the ox's bridle. A couple of men were loading the wagon with crates, trunks and hat boxes. An uncomfortable feeling of intruding crept through Ida. She'd state her business and get away as quickly as possible.

Ida brought Old Molly to a stop near Jared, who was standing on his daughter's side of the surrey. Her heart hit bottom at the adoring look he gave his daughter before turning to greet her. It was as plain as the nose on a face that any woman wanting to get close to the father would need the daughter's approval. From the look Kate gave her as she drove up, there was no way she'd get that approval.

Jared stepped toward Ida's wagon. "Kate and her grandmother are leaving for a stay in Sheridan."

"I won't take much of your time." Her voice sounded tight as she held Old Molly in check. "If this wasn't an emergency, I wouldn't intrude."

He frowned. "What's wrong?"

"Clear Creek's rising dangerously. Could you divert water over your meadows? It might save my crops."

She wondered how he'd respond with his daughter looking on. Her censorious glare sent shivers up and down Ida's arms.

"I'll talk with Russ and see what we can do."

Gratitude flowed through Ida.

"Much obliged," she said—and saying "walk on" to Old Molly, she got herself out of there.

* * * *

"Why ever did you say you'd help that woman, Father?" his daughter asked even before Ida's wagon passed out of earshot. She smoothed her skirts with an angry gesture. "You need to protect our property, not hers." Kate sounded exasperated.

Why had he agreed so readily? In the past, he'd have thought longer before committing to help. He was coming to see the world from Ida's point of view. He could still back out. He could say the task was impossible. But he didn't want to.

"I'm helping a neighbor in times of trouble."

"A neighbor you wouldn't have said 'good morning' to a couple of months ago," Kate said, "and you know it." Her mouth took on a pronounced pout.

Jared lost sympathy with his daughter. "I've learned that Mrs. Osterbach's a fine woman," he said, stiffly. "And hard-working."

"You like her." Kate sounded as if tears would flow. "You'll forget about my mother!"

His heart skipped beats. He had no idea Kate worried about her mother being supplanted in his affections. "Your mother will always have a special place in my heart."

Kate pressed her lips into a grim line. "So you say now."

"I'm reminded of her every time I look at you," Jared said.

His daughter's face scrunched into a fit of ire. She balled her fists. "Let her take care of her own darn farm."

"Kate, dear," her grandmother said with sternness. "A lady never swears and never discusses family business in front of the hired help."

Kate looked at her grandmother, her face flushing red. "But—"

Mrs. Evan's put a finger on her granddaughter's lips. "A man has a right to live his life as he chooses. It's not our place to meddle. Besides, ranching is men's business. Women shouldn't interfere."

She turned to her son-in-law. "I'll take good care of my dear granddaughter. Send word when it's safe to return." Waving a hand at the coachman, she said, "Driver, let's be on our way."

The man climbed onto the driver's seat and flicked the reins. The fringed surrey left at a good clip. The creaking ox-drawn wagon laden with luggage followed more slowly. With unease, Jared watched their departure until the diminishing outline of his daughter could no longer be made out.

* * * *

Later that morning, Jared and Russ were at the meandering creek, trying to decide what could reasonably be done to divert water away from Ida's farm.

"I don't see where we can do much," Russ was saying as they stood on the ridge of the bank staring at the obviously rising waters. "Looks like we'll have a struggle ourselves."

"There must be something we can do."

"The problem is the land slopes toward her farm," Russ said. "If we divert some of it over the meadow, the water will eventually get to her anyway."

"What about ditches?"

Russ ran his fingers through his hair. "Maybe. I'd been considering digging a pond down here for the horses." He discussed the logistics of his idea.

"Round up the men you can spare," Jared said, "and hire more from town. I want to get that pond dug before the creek overflows."

Re-mounting, he said, "I think I'll swing over to the farm to let Ida know what we're doing."

Russ looked at him. "Ida, is it? And here I thought you couldn't stomach the woman."

Jared drew himself up as he sat his horse. "We had a chance to converse the other week. She's an intelligent woman." He sounded officious even to himself.

It hadn't been lost on him that both Kate and her grandmother considered a farmer woman beneath their social scale. Still, he couldn't get out of his mind how fine Ida looked today in her flowered dress. Perhaps—while his daughter was gone—he'd invite her over for sherry and a tour of his library. She might even stay for supper.

Chapter 16

The worst possible combinations of weather were happening. By mid-week, the water level was rising—
frighteningly.

The unusual ground-level April heat clashed with cold,
high mountain air causing violent thunderstorms. Five days
of storms melted the nine thousand feet high snow pack. At
ground level, intense summer thunderstorms with sharp
lightning and pelting rain produced devastating flash floods.
Although most of Wyoming was arid, its mountainous re-
gions could average more than sixty inches of rain per year.
Ida felt like the whole year's worth fell at once on her farm.

Even at the highest barriers Ernest and the hands had
constructed, the creek overflowed. Everyone, including Peggy, was knee-deep in mud, struggling to make a section of
the embankment higher yet to keep the waters from totally
flooding the road and blocking off their route to town and
supplies.

The farmhouse and barn buildings were well above the
flood line at the top of a slight rise so that Ida didn't worry
about them. The road, their escape route, was a major con-

cern. The creek paralleled the road for about a mile. If that whole section got underwater, it could take weeks for the water to recede and the mud to dry enough for a wagon to pull through it.

Pelting rain stoned her face and stung her lower arms where her sleeves rode up exposing unprotected skin. She was drenched and shivering. The creek's mad rush was throwing all kinds of refuse against the embankment, including dead animals that hadn't been able to find shelter against the storms.

"We're not making much progress, cousin," Ernest yelled over the force of the storm. "It's getting too dangerous."

Jared, who was working at Ida's shoulder, agreed. "Next thing you know one of us will be swept away."

Her shoulders sagged. She hated giving up. It wasn't in her nature. But they were right. It had become impossible to protect the roadway and themselves as well. She had to choose. Better to get inside where it was warm and dry and hunker down. She couldn't forge on and make someone sick from being knee deep in water.

"Let's get back to the house."

In just five days, the crops they planted these last months were submerged in flood waters. She'd fought as long and as hard as she could. Nature wore her down. Nature compelled her surrender where Beau Campbell could not.

* * * *

Several days later, Jared lingered at the ranch house dinner table with Russ. He was savoring this respite, having been out most of the day dealing with storm damage. Sadie brought a fresh pot of coffee and left the brandy decanter and the crystal glasses on the table.

"The cattle were still on high ground," Russ was telling Jared. "We may have lost some calves, but the main stock should be fine. Too dangerous to go and check. The rain gutted the trails. The ground's still unstable."

Jared nodded, glad to be in dry clothes.

"We'll see how things go tomorrow. It may've dried out enough," Russ said.

"I'm worried about Ida Osterbach. With the creek overflowing, she must be trapped in the farmhouse."

"Nothin' you can do about it," Russ said. "Too treacherous."

"Only worry."

* * * *

The following week on Sunday morning, Ida sat with Jared in her kitchen drinking chicory coffee. They were alone. Peggy was at the barn feeding the chickens and the men were out making storm repairs. He'd ridden over to see her—the first opportunity to travel safely between the two homesteads. The storms were over. The waters were receding. The road to town was becoming passable by wagon.

The chicory's bitterness matched her mood. With her crops under water and rotting, there was no way she could pay her mortgage. The debris created by the storm and carried by the raging waters had rooted out many feet of fencing and carried away a shed. Muddy water sat four inches deep in her newly planted fields. Her breathing quickened. She fiddled with the ruffle running down the front of her dress. "I'm ruined."

Deep sadness brought shortness of breath. She forced out words she'd never thought she'd say. Each word was like a death sentence. "You...can...buy...me...out."

Jared surprised her by enveloping her in a bear hug. She mumbled into his shirt pocket, "I can't go on."

He sat back and banged the kitchen table with the flat of his hand. "You can't give up."

She stared at him with disbelief. "The fields are submerged."

If she were the crying type, this is where she'd be bawling. "I'll have no crop this year. I won't even have enough money to survive the winter." She chewed her lower lip before speaking. "A partial loss, I could survive. Total, no."

"You don't have to sell," he said.

"How do you figure that?"

"If we can get enough water off the fields, you may be able to save some crops."

"How?"

"Your land slopes to the creek. I'll get some of the boys to work with Ernest and your hands to pull apart that barrier you built. The fields will drain on their own."

The tightness around her heart started melting away. With enough men, it could work. She caught herself up short with a sobering thought. "I don't have the money to pay your workers. I barely have money for lumber and fencing."

"Let me worry about that."

"I don't like to be beholden."

"For God's sake, woman," Jared growled, "I'm just being neighborly."

She must have looked alarmed because he added more mildly, "Come harvest time, you can be neighborly and pay me back with fresh vegetables."

"But," she said, needing to understand, "you wanted to buy me out two years ago. I thought you'd jump at the chance."

"That was before I knew you."

His words took her aback. Had so much changed these last months? "What's different?"

"Back then, I thought no woman should be running a farm," he said. "I thought you should put Ernest in charge and move into town."

Those days seemed so long ago. She laughed, apologetically. "Your high-handedness got my back up so often I could barely be civil."

"I've changed." A rueful expression crossed his face. "You deserve to own the farm. You're courageous and industrious. I'll help you keep it."

"Draining that water will give me a chance."

"I'll do more than that," Jared said. "I'll guarantee your mortgage until you can catch up."

Her breathing collapsed in upon itself. Suspicions resurfaced. It didn't make sense. Why call her crop loan and then offer to back her mortgage?

"But your bank just called my crop loan."

A flash of anger crossed his face. His body tensed. "The bank did *what*?"

Her breathing was constricted. She cocked her head to one side, frowned and issued an accusation. "Is this your way to take over my farm and not have to buy me out? Will you suddenly withdraw your support and put me into foreclosure?"

Jared puckered his eyebrows, looking puzzled, then angry. "What are you talking about, woman? I'm trying to save your farm!"

Her eyes, like slits, accused him. Her temper rose as she spoke. "How can I trust you? Your bank called my crop loan. That call put me into a financial bind."

Jared's face reddened. "I know nothing about a call. I'm a major stockholder, but I don't run it day-to-day."

She wanted to believe him.

"I'm on the board. Why wasn't I told?" The way he said it was like he was talking to himself.

Ida's temper was receding. "If the bank hadn't called the loan, I wouldn't be short of cash for repairs."

A scowl darkened Jared's face. "An early call makes no sense. Everybody knows farmers don't have money until after harvests."

"I have until the end of this month," she said. "I have the money, but with the flooding, I haven't gotten to town to pay it."

"Don't pay. I'll get to the bottom of this." Jared ran his fingers through his hair, roughing it up and making strands stick out awkwardly. "I'll ride to town Monday and find out what's going on. There has to be a mistake."

"I'd have money to rebuild the sheds if I can wait until harvest to pay the loan; that is, assuming the fields drain as expected."

"I'll see to it the bank doesn't foreclose on you."

Ida mentally pinched herself as a heavy burden rolled

off her shoulders. Just when everything seemed lost, an unlikely angel had rescued her.

"I can't thank you enough for saving my farm."

"We haven't saved your farm yet. I need to round up the men." Jared pushed back the chair, picked up his Stetson and put it on his head on his way out the kitchen door. Hope for her future went with him.

He left her sitting at her kitchen table feeling like a tornado had blown through her emotions.

Chapter 17

Jared didn't bother with banker's clothes when he rode to town after breakfast on Monday. He'd just come off the range, having left at daybreak with Russ to check on how the cattle were settling down after the flood. He wanted to be back from town quickly to supervise the repair of washed-out trails.

As he entered the Main Street door of the bank located next to the Occidental Hotel, he didn't take the time like he usually did to appreciate the high-ceilinged rooms with their rich colors and brass fittings. He didn't even extract his usual pleasure from the low hum of business and the efficient rustle of papers.

When he spotted Frank Larson at his substantial desk in a rear office containing the walk-in vault, he walked straight back. The clerks offered greetings as he passed. Often, he'd take time to chat, but not today. Other things occupied his mind. He wanted to resolve Ida's problems and get back to ranch business.

Knocking sharply on the frame of the opened doorway, he immediately entered and closed the office door behind himself. He didn't want to expose Ida's business to the curiosity of the depositors.

"Sorry to intrude, Frank, but I'm on a tight schedule today. I want to get to the bottom of something before more time passes."

Larson rose slightly, smiled and waved him to a chair as he spoke. "Always at your service."

Jared sat. "I'll take care of this and be on my way."

"No rush on my part. How is your lovely daughter?"

He'd assumed Larson would ask about Kate and had decided to modify the reasons for her departure so that the man wouldn't ask questions. "She and her grandmother are taking an extended vacation. They've settled in at the Sheridan Inn for several months."

A look of disappointment crossed the banker's face. His smile was having a hard time staying in place. "Please send my regards when you next communicate with them." He carefully clasped his hands on the uncluttered desk pad of the mahogany desk as if it were his way of re-gathering his thoughts. "Now, what may I do for you?"

"I'm here on behalf of my neighbor, Mrs. Osterbach."

Larson's smile faded. A look as if he'd swallowed vinegar replaced it, leaving Jared puzzled.

"She was hit hard by the flooding," he continued. "There's no telling how much of the crop was lost. We know one of her sheep drowned."

Larson continued to look like he'd swallowed the canary and Jared was beginning to wonder about the man.

"I want to guarantee Mrs. Osterbach's mortgage until she can get on her feet."

Relief passed over the banker's face. "Certainly, Jared. That can be arranged. You've done it for so many others in town. It's only right that you help your neighbor. I'll have the clerk prepare the form." He rose quickly and stepped outside to confer with a man seated at a nearby desk.

Jared watched through the open door as the bank clerk went through a file drawer of forms until he found a particular one. He showed it to Larson, who nodded in agreement and returned to his office, shutting the door behind himself.

"It will be no time at all to have the form prepared. May I offer you some refreshment while you wait?" The banker indicated a tray of rolls on a small credenza.

Jared waved his hand in dismissal. "I've already had breakfast. Besides, I have one more piece of business. It seems Mrs. Osterbach's crop loan was called in early."

Larson's face paled.

"Why did that happen?" Jared's voice demanded answers.

"Well...you see...that is..." For a man fluid in language, Larson was having a hard time finding words.

"Are we doing that to other farmers? Has the bank changed its policy?"

The banker shook his head. "No, no, no. It was a unique case."

"Unique? What's unique about a crop loan?"

"That is...I mean..."

Jared gave Larson his fiercest scowl. "The call of her loan is putting her in a financial bind, especially with unexpected expenses due to the flooding. I want to get to the bottom of this."

"There were special circumstances…" Larson seemed to have lost all of his banker's cockiness and replaced it with backpedaling. Jared had no idea why.

"I'd prefer the call be withdrawn, but if it isn't, I'll cover it."

"Um, another party is involved. I'm not sure I can withdraw it."

"Who bought out the loan?"

"Well…it's not exactly a buy out." Larson looked guilty and Jared was getting angry.

"Then, what is it?" he snapped.

"I try to keep transactions confidential."

"What the devil is going on here? I'm on the board. I demand to know." Jared slapped his hand against the arm rest of his chair, making Larson jump.

The banker swallowed hard. "Well, sir, it was a favor for your daughter."

Jared's insides felt like they'd been reamed out. "*Kate* was behind this? Kate did this?"

"Well, not exactly, Sir." Larson was wringing his hands. "We were talking at the Occidental the other week—"

"My daughter put you up to this loan call?" Jared interrupted.

The banker nodded. "She's very afraid some woman will supplant her mother. She wanted to give Mrs. Osterbach something to think about besides you."

Stunned, Jared's breath seemed sucked out of his body. Had that fancy school back East purged his daughter's sense of decency? Where else could she have been taught to manipulate?

Larson was wringing his hands. "She was in such distress…that is, in my small way I hoped to…"

If she weren't already out of town, Jared would have throttled her.

Larson interrupted his thoughts. "I was the one who suggested the crop loan. After all, the bank has every right to ask for its money."

Jared jumped up, roughly pushing his wooden chair out of the way and scraping it along the floor. He spoke through clenched teeth. "I want that call reversed. If there is no other purpose behind it except my daughter's wish, I want it reversed."

"Of course, Sir."

"When would you normally have collected?"

"After the harvest."

Jared glared at Larson. "See to it that a letter is sent as early as possible to Mrs. Osterbach putting the loan back on its original footing."

"But your daughter…"

"Leave my daughter to me. You see to the letter."

Until his temper cooled, it was just as well Kate was out of town. There was much she did that he forgave. This might not be one of them.

He heard Larson's quiet, "Yes, Sir," as he stormed out of the banker's office and past the clerk's cubbyhole.

The clerk ran after him. "Sir. Your form. It's ready for you to sign."

Jared snatched the legal envelope out of the clerk's hand.

"I'll deal with it later." Tucking the envelope containing

the mortgage guarantee form into his pant pocket, Jared swiftly left the bank, his mind in turmoil.

* * * *

Jared rode his horse harder than was wise and did soul-searching as he rode homeward after his meeting with Larson. Muscles bunched in his thighs as the gelding loped the flood-rutted road. The mount snorted, its tongue hung out and its breathing sounded heavy. Realizing he was traveling too fast, Jared reined to a canter. He didn't need to break his neck before arriving at the Bar J work party in the foothills.

That his beloved daughter caused Ida's loan troubles was sinking in. By neither word nor gesture did Kate reveal her underhandedness before leaving for Sheridan. Surely, she should've shown some guilt. Jared recalled her excitement about traveling and found none.

He mulled over what had been revealed at the bank. It was easier for him to take on some of the blame rather than think of his daughter as vindictive. Perhaps his own angry response to Ida's refusal to sell upon her husband's death had given Kate the impression that he'd welcome seeing the woman in financial difficulty. Or was it truly his very recent change toward Ida that convinced his daughter their neighbor was supplanting her mother in his affections? He could see where his daughter might think so.

He slowed the horse to a trot.

It was well past time to be thinking about a companion for his declining years. Although he couldn't expect a great love like with Isabella, he certainly could expect a companionable woman to manage his household. Images of an efficiently run farm entered his mind. Currently, his mother-in-law oversaw the running of his household. When his daughter married, she would leave to run Kate's establishment. Her departure would leave the oversight of his own ranch house to hired staff—unless he married again.

Just before the Bar J entrance gate, Jared cut to the right. The cross-country trail led directly to the work party in the hills. Once there, he joined Russ in organizing and assisting the men in clearing washed-out trails of mud slides and fallen trees. The dilemma that was his daughter and Ida was pushed to the back of his mind as he worked, but refused to be totally routed.

By the time they set up the mid-day camp fire to heat the coffee and beef stew sent from the ranch house, Jared had exhausted himself—but Kate's actions still dominated his thoughts. He drew Russ to one side to unburden himself while they ate. Jared explained the crop loan circumstances.

"I'm surprised Miss Kate is worried," Russ said. "She knows you adored her mother."

"She wasn't spiteful as a child. I don't know where this comes from."

Russ chuckled. "She's grown now. She understands her effect on a man and how to use it to her benefit."

"It's hard for me to accept," Jared said. "I know she's grown, but she's still my little girl."

"Larson certainly gave her what she wanted," Russ said.

Jared shook his head, wearily. He needed to talk with his daughter. "If the roads are good enough, I'll ride over to Sheridan this weekend and have it out with her."

"Don't forget Mrs. Osterbach," Russ said. "You owe her an explanation."

"I'll go over there the first chance I get."

* * * *

That Wednesday night, Jared reined in his black stallion near the wooden rail at the farm's water trough. Hank offered to rub down the winded horse and Jared gratefully surrendered the reins.

Having been busy with flood repairs, this was his first opportunity to let Ida know about his daughter's hand in the crop loan debacle.

He crossed the packed earth toward the farmhouse. He was negotiating the porch steps two at a time when the woman occupying his thoughts opened the front door and stepped out. She looked magnificent in a brightly colored, gingham dress, with a long, dark-blue shawl covering her shoulders. She must've rubbed scented oil into her skin since an aroma of lilacs clung to her. The deep desire he felt at the church musical re-stirred itself. His eyes lingered where the gingham stretched tightly across a generous bosom.

He wanted to hold her in his arms to assure himself she was all right. He wanted to pledge to protect her always from floods and loan calls. He wanted to tell her that he would keep her safe. He did none of those.

"Good evening, Mr. Buell," she said with a smile.

He touched his hat in greeting. "Are you all right?"

She nodded. "We're slowly climbing out from under the wreckage. The fields have drained and we'll salvage something."

"Good."

"Mr. Larson drove out and personally apologized for

the error that resulted in my crop loan being called."

"Good."

"Did the flood do much damage at the ranch?" she asked. "I was so preoccupied with my own troubles last Sunday that I never asked."

"Quite a bit, but we've got it mostly under control."

"Good," she said.

There was silence while he struggled with how to begin to tell her about his daughter's treachery. He shuffled his feet while he considered words.

"I was about to take a stroll," she said, thankfully interrupting his mental deliberations. "Care to join me?"

He swept off his Stetson and gave Ida a courtly bow. "My pleasure."

He wasn't a man for courtly bows—he left those to the prissy town fellows. He broke horses and herded cattle. Embarrassed, he put his high-crowned hat back on his head and dampened down his enthusiasm by remembering his purpose for being here. Reluctantly, he got to the matter at hand.

"I need to talk with you about that loan call."

"Can we speak as we walk?" she asked.

"Certainly."

Offering his arm, he escorted her down the porch steps. Ida wrapped her arm tightly through his, bringing their bodies so close that their hips brushed.

He pointed out some jagged stones. "Be careful. Don't trip."

It was ridiculous to believe Ida wouldn't have noticed the stones washed up onto the lane when the creek overflowed. After all, she walked in rutted fields at all hours of the day and night. But the role of protector was a satisfying one—even while he knew that protecting her was none of his business. Ida would surely remind him if he overstepped the boundary.

Unlike Isabella—whose petite frame had made Jared feel awkward—Ida matched him in size. In fact, her height so perfectly matched his that he could easily rest her head on his shoulder. He imaged her lying beside him, her head on his shoulder and her hair spread out around her.

"I have something to confess." He dragged his mind away from carnal thoughts.

"What, pray tell?"

"It involves my daughter…" He felt her tense up. "…and the call." She calmed as if that burden had been dissolved.

"Thanks to you, I've been saved from that loan call. And Mr. Larson said that, with your guarantee, I don't have to worry about the mortgage."

"I'm glad, but—"

She interrupted. "I've been counting my blessings all day. I don't know how to thank you enough."

Optimism was her driving force—a trait he admired—but she shouldn't be grateful to him. His daughter was the cause of the problem.

"That call never should have happened," he started again.

"So Mr. Larson told me."

"My daughter…that is, Frank Larson…"

"You don't have to say any more," she said. "Mr. Larson explained everything. It had nothing to do with the flood or a change of bank policy."

"And you're not angry with me?" he asked.

"Why should I be? You didn't know."

"I didn't."

"You had no way of preventing it."

Relief flooded through him. Larson had resolved the issue. He was spared exposing the details of Kate's spitefulness.

Ida smiled up at him as they walked. "Just to remind myself I can survive anything, I washed from head to toe tonight and put on one of my good dresses."

Jared would've liked to have been there for the head to toe. He found himself leaning toward her and being rewarded by a whiff of lilacs.

The air carried the aromas of plowed earth and new growth. A full moon lighted a roadbed dried out from the recent flooding. Fluffy white cottonwood balls—blown off nearby trees—covered the ground. Normally, he'd be annoyed at these for sticking to his boots. Tonight, he found nothing annoying.

"Aren't the night sounds soothing?" she asked.

Unaware of them, Jared tuned in to the sounds of insects and birds and found them the same as always—neither soothing nor annoying.

"Very," he lied.

They came to the place where the creek paralleled the road.

"Would you like to sit under that willow for a while and listen to the creek?" she asked. "If it's still damp, we can sit on my shawl."

"Won't you get cold?"

He mentally kicked himself for opening a reason for not sitting beneath the tree. More than anything, he wanted to sit in the shadows next to this enticing woman.

"I don't really need the shawl."

Relieved, Jared guided her to the willow whose branches dipped close to the earth. He pulled aside boughs to make a doorway for her to enter. As nonchalantly as possible—considering his rapidly beating heart and clumsy fingers—Jared raised the shawl off her shoulders and spread it at the trunk of the tree. He offered her a hand. With surprising gracefulness for so big a woman, she gathered her skirts, accepted his hand and slipped downward onto the shawl. Jared folded his long frame against the solid trunk of the willow and took the bold step of slipping an arm around her shoulders.

"This is pleasant," he heard Ida say through the fog of emotions she stirred within him.

"Good," he answered.

Heat flowed into him where her hip rested against his. Ida startled him by resting her head on his shoulder. Thick brunette hair pushed against his chin and tickled the underside of his nose. With reluctance, he pushed it away.

"Is there a problem?"

"Not really. Your braid was tickling my nose."

"My hair's been bothering me tonight."

When she lifted her head off his shoulder, he was sorry he'd brushed the strands aside that had tickled his nose.

"Sometimes the braid pulls on my roots." She leaned forward and began pulling out hair pins and dropping them into her lap. "It's a blessing to let my hair down."

"Let me help."

Jared couldn't believe he'd made the impudent suggestion, but his hands were already searching eagerly through her thick hair. He removed pins by feel since little of the moon's light got through the willow's branches. He hadn't touched a woman's hair since Isabella passed. He'd forgotten how soft it felt, even to his callused hands.

Heat poured from Ida's lower body when he dropped the hair pins into her lap. While withdrawing his hand, he briefly and deliberately touched her waist. The flesh was firm, curving outward into the swell of her hip.

He worked steadily, his hands trembling as he invaded the silky strands. When he reached around Ida to drop more pins into her lap, he accidentally brushed against her bosom. His breath caught, making it hard to swallow.

"Pardon me."

He could think of nothing further to say, so he said nothing more.

She shifted and turned toward him.

"If you wouldn't find it unseemly, I could sit in front of you, between your legs. Then you could work straight on."

A wish come true. "It'll save me from sitting at an awkward angle." His voice sounded strained to his ears.

Ida swept the metal pins from her lap and into her hand. She scrambled to her feet. Jared shifted to the center of the shawl. He leaned against the tree trunk so he could support both their weights. When Ida re-settled herself, she kept a disappointing couple of inches between their bodies.

Just as well, he acknowledged. He was experiencing a

swelling that Ida should know nothing about.

After he removed the last of the pins and she put them in a pocket, Jared started unbraiding the strands of lilac-scented hair. He rolled the folded end of the braid between his fingers to remove the piece of hair binding it. He inserted two fingers into the braiding and slowly pulled the strands apart. Heat rose up his spine. Intellectually, he knew his only task was unbraiding a woman's hair. Yet, there was a tightening in his loins that he hadn't experienced in years.

With each unwinding of the braid, he ran his fingers through the long strands to release the knots. Soft hair brushed the backs of his hands as he probed the lilac-scented braid falling to the curve in her back. He worked upward, his knuckles occasionally resting against her supple spine.

Ida sat quietly as he worked. Now and then, he thought he detected a soft sigh rise above the murmurs of the creek water.

He loosened several inches and was gaining on her shoulder blades—infinitely aware that a splendid bosom resided on the other side. His breathing seemed labored as if he'd run a long distance. On reaching the nape of her neck, he paused to brush aside her hair. Impulsively, he kissed the white skin revealed above the gingham fabric. Ida stiffened, but then relaxed.

Jared brought his mind back to his task. He finished the unbraiding and ran his hands underneath the long hair to spread it across her shoulders. He wished he could see his handiwork clearly, but it was far too dim under the willow.

"Done," he said.

"That feels much better."

Drawing her backward into an embrace, he nuzzled the scented skin beneath her ear lobe before resting his chin on the top of her head. Cuddling this way, they listened to the sounds of the creek. Before long, Jared's restless hands started roving, tracing the curve of her waistline. His fingers inched upward until they rested happily against the undersides of her weighty breasts. She made no move to push him away.

Still unsatisfied, he pushed her long hair to one side to kiss the nape of her neck and continued upward until he reached the corner of her mouth. He drew her chin toward himself until her full lips were his for the taking. His body reverberated with the intense emotions flowing through him.

Pausing only long enough for a breath, he plunged into the softness of her mouth. With a hunger he hadn't experienced in years, he kissed this stubborn farmer until his lungs cried out for air. He must get her clothes off.

Tiny, cloth-covered buttons held the gingham dress together from its neckline to below Ida's navel. Working blindly from behind, he clumsily made a frustratingly slow way downward. He had three buttons undone when he realized Ida was helping. She'd undone the buttons covering her breasts. He eagerly slipped his hand into the opening, cradling the weight of a breast through her cotton petticoat. Blood pounded in his temples. He was afire. No ingénue here, but an experienced widow, a mature woman equaling his passion.

Jared lowered Ida onto the shawl and worked on his trouser buttons.

Even the shock of cooling night air couldn't diminish

his desire as he pushed away confining trousers and unbuttoned his long johns. Ida had pushed up her petticoat. His
body felt like a coiled spring on the cusp of springing free as
he untied and pushed down her cotton bloomers. Her tongue
sought his even as his fingers explored between her legs.
Their heavy breathing rose into the night air.

As he eased himself inside, she cried out and wrapped
her legs around him—urging him deeper into her moist
depths. Her rhythm was patterned by Nature. Tension spiraled ever higher until he gasped for air and exploded. The
world became a pattern of multicolored lights behind closed
eyelids which gradually receded into blackness.

Drained—feeling like the most satiated man on earth—
it took several minutes before Jared had the strength of mind
to ask Ida if she was all right. Guilt crept in. He shouldn't
have let his own urgency blind him to her needs. "Are you
all right," he asked again.

* * * *

Am I all right?

She savored the sensations of a physical release in a
grateful body, dormant these past years. Before committing
herself, she'd fleetingly worried she'd be betraying Dean—
but that hadn't happened. Instead, it was as if her beloved
were telling her it was about time.

"I am," she assured Jared. "And you?"

"I've not felt this good in years." He sat up, stretched,
and reached for his discarded clothing.

The curve of his lower spine—visible where a sliver of
moonlight worked its way through the branches—beckoned
to her. She reached out and ran her fingers over the hard

ridges. Jared twisted around to kiss her. They dressed leisurely, at ease with one another.

For years she'd cold-shouldered this man. Only weeks
ago, her biggest terror was making small talk at the church
hall. Tonight carried them beyond their prejudices—
permanently changing them. When she'd committed to the
walk down the dark road and suggested the seclusion of the
willow tree, she had no idea the result would be this great.

"I think we should get married," she heard him say.

Ida stiffened—a proposal of marriage was the last thing
she expected. It would never work, of course. Logic told her
so.

Yes, they'd changed—but not that radically that the
change could be the foundation for a happy marriage.

For heaven's sakes, she thought, *we've been neighbors for
years with nothing much to say to one another. He's a rancher
with a spoilt daughter whose eyes shoot daggers at me. I'm a
farmer who won't throw away my life's work for a night of
good loving. They needed time—time to become companions
before exploring anything deeper—time to heal the rancor of
the past. Besides, she was happy as she was. A few visits like
this each month and some social occasions to relax and get
away from farm chores would be enough for her.*

Jared waited, looking at her questioningly. She needed
words that would preserve their new-found friendship while
still denying him. She needed obstacles—something to show
how impossible the idea was.

"Marriage is more than physical desire."

"I agree," he said, obligingly. "I admire your courage,
your determination."

"We both have people depending on us."

Jared nodded, once again annoyingly agreeing. "Marriage doesn't mean we forget about others. Nor that we neglect our responsibilities."

Frustration rose.

"We both had spouses we loved deeply. Those memories are hard to set aside."

Jared put his hands on her shoulders and looked her in the eye. "They'd want us to move on. You know they'd want that for us."

She did.

"Your daughter doesn't like me," she said in desperation.

Jared frowned. "She doesn't like very many people. She's been spoiled. She'll come around when she gets to know you."

And pigs will fly, Ida thought.

"She wouldn't want another woman stepping into her mother's position."

"It's not her life," he said gruffly. "It's mine. Besides, she'll soon marry and set up her own establishment."

Ida needed a clean break—but one that didn't shatter their fragile friendship. She searched frantically for another reason not to marry—one that he'd accept. Tension made her voice sound strangled. "But...but," she stuttered, "we have to...that is, before making a decision this big, we must consider that others..."

He cut her off with a finger to her lips.

"Other people can take care of themselves. This is about us, Ida. Besides, I shouldn't have taken advantage of you. You've had enough to contend with of late."

That caught her up short—he was worried about her reputation. Instead of love, his proposal was a duty. Although she'd been searching for reasons not to marry, she couldn't stop the disappointment that swam into her gut when she realized that his motives were chivalrous.

"I knew what I was doing." She forced the words through tight lips. "I'm not an inexperienced debutante. Besides, widows have more relaxed rules. I don't need you to protect my honor. I can protect that myself."

Jared shook his head. "That's not the point. Well, in one way it is. But the main point is that you woke me up from the lethargy I'd slipped into after Isabella's death. I haven't felt this good in years. For that, I want you near me—always."

Not exactly words of love—more like selfish desire. Still, it was something. She'd had great love with Dean. Companionship with Jared would do—if only there weren't so many barriers.

Tension grew. She needed time to think. She needed time to figure out how to resolve some of these problems that could easily destroy a companionable union. She needed time to make his love deeper so that it could withstand the challenges.

He took her in his arms. When he nuzzled her neck, he created marvelous sensations throughout her body.

"We can see each other without marriage." Unintentionally, her voice was almost a whisper.

Jared exhaled, sounding highly exasperated. She hastened to reassure him.

"It's not like I'd never want to marry. Once we work things out—"

He interrupted. "I think we should announce our court-ship—start making wedding plans."

She threw her hands up in exasperation. "I need time." Her voice was tinged with anger. "I need time to make sure that marriage is right for me."

Jared drew her against the length of his body and cupped her head into his shoulder. The yearning in him reached out and enveloped her.

Ida spoke into his shirt pocket to a rhythm set by the steady beat of his heart. "It feels right at this moment," she murmured, "but will it stay right? There are so many obsta-cles."

He bent to nuzzle the side of her neck, his breath warm on her skin. "You're a stubborn woman, Ida Osterbach."

Roiling desire surfaced forcefully when he left a trail of kisses along her neck. His hands glided down her back and stroked her buttocks.

"Are you certain I can't change your mind? Are you certain you want to pass this up?"

Ida slipped her arms around his strong neck, urgently seeking his lips. Soon her breath was coming hard and fast. Between kisses she managed to gasp out, "Perhaps a long courtship would work."

Chapter 18

It was Saturday morning, almost a week since Jared's confrontation at the bank with Frank Larson. He was riding down the main street in Sheridan and he'd calmed down about the loan call. The tension he felt across his shoulders was because he needed to tell Kate he was replacing her mother with a new wife. How she'd react when he gave her the news was more than he could contemplate.

Jared recognized some of the men seated on benches and rockers spread along the broad veranda of the newly built hotel, famous for its sixty-nine gables. Located on the corner of Fifth Street and Broadway in Sheridan, the Inn's veranda ran the full length of its front. Jared's friend, Colonel William F. "Buffalo Bill" Cody, was part owner. The hotel was the famous entertainer's home whenever he was in town, but Jared didn't see him among the men scattered about the long porch. Even though Jared begrudged the distraction, he felt obliged to stop and chat with a few men near the door before entering the lobby where his daughter and his mother-in-law would be waiting.

As quickly as possible, he said goodbye to those acquaintances. He removed his Stetson and stepped into the hotel lobby. His beautiful daughter and decorous mother-in-law were seated on the red velvet sofa across from the registration desk.

"Father." Kate gave a quick wave of her hand to catch his attention. She was a vision in a yellow frock with white polka-dots and all the eyes in the room were aware of her. His heart swelled with pride that he was her father. Only his mission dampened his pleasure.

"What an unexpected delight!" Kate trilled. "You could've knocked me over with a feather when you sent word you were coming."

"I know this is unexpected," he said.

"And it's a good thing you let me know, too. We wouldn't have been here if you hadn't. We were invited to a garden party this afternoon." She pouted a little. "I sent our regrets."

Jared bent to kiss his daughter's cheek and then his mother-in-law's before saying, "I trust you are well."

"In fine spirits," Mrs. Evan said.

"I have something to tell you. Let's go out and take a walk along the boardwalk so we're not overheard."

"What is it?" Kate asked.

"I've had a talk with Frank Larson."

His daughter's face took on a guarded look.

"Do you want me with you, Jared," his mother-in-law asked, "or should I stay here?"

He thought briefly and decided to include her. "It's probably best if you walked with us. You should know what happened."

"What are you accusing me of?" Kate's voice rose so loud the hotel guests checking in at the reception desk looked her way.

He took his daughter's upper arm to bring her to her feet. "Let's continue this outside."

She jerked her arm free, but led the way through the door and toward the Fifth Street boardwalk. Her grandmother clutched a colorful parasol with end ruffles and hurried after Kate. Jared brought up the rear.

"I do wish you'd brought your parasol, dearest," Mrs. Evans said as she opened hers against the strong mid-day sun. "Your skin will redden."

"I don't care," Kate flung back over her shoulder. "I have cream to correct that."

"Not sufficient for long-term damage," her grandmother said. "Prevention is best."

Eventually, they sorted themselves out on the walkway. Jared stepped between the two women and offered each an arm. Mrs. Evans accepted. His daughter did not.

Jared shortened his stride to compensate for his mother-in-law's shorter steps. At times like this, he especially appreciated that Ida could match his full stride. That allowed him to be himself and not mince about like he was doing today.

"Now, what's this all about?" his mother-in-law asked when they were well out of earshot. "I don't understand the urgency. What made you make the long trip over here?"

Although he was answering his mother-in-law's question, Jared looked at his daughter.

"I talked with Frank Larson on Monday. He told me

that you, Kate, were the one who put the idea in his head for the call of the Osterbach crop loan."

His daughter halted to stamp her foot. "How could he say such a thing?"

"Why would you even bring that idea up?" Jared asked, a puzzled frown creasing his forehead. "I don't understand how Mrs. Osterbach's mortgage got into a conversation of yours in the first place."

"Well, it happened that Sunday after church when we had lunch at the hotel. You'd complained the night before about my speaking with Mr. Campbell." Kate's chin quivered with indignation. "Yet, I saw you and that farmer woman talking with him right there by your table in the Occidental."

"That wasn't a friendly conversation."

"How was I to know?" Kate asked with a shrug. "I was angry, that's all. What's good for the goose should have been good for the gander."

"Still—"

"I may have said words that I shouldn't have said, but if Mr. Larson took me seriously, that's his fault."

Jared studied his daughter He wanted desperately to believe her. "He told me he understood your intention."

"How unkind of him to cast dispersions on dear Kate," Mrs. Evans said. "I'll have to reevaluate my understanding of the man."

"He told me he suggested the crop loan," Jared said, "because a change in mortgage terms, like you suggested, must come before the board, but a crop loan doesn't."

"See? His idea, not mine," Kate said.

"The crop loan was indeed his idea," Mrs. Evans said, reinforcing the point.

"I told you so." Kate placed her hands on her hips and looked like she was ready to stamp her foot.

"I was there, Jared," his mother-in-law said in conciliatory tones. "Her actions were unladylike, but not to be taken seriously."

"I told you so."

"I reprimanded her," Mrs. Evans said. "Mr. Larson should have known I wouldn't tolerate such behavior."

Jared's voice became serious. "Larson actually called the loan."

"He didn't!" Mrs. Evans looked aghast. "How could he be that stupid?"

Jared was feeling more uncertainty about the accuracy of the banker's statements. His mother-in-law must be right. It must have been a big misunderstanding. It could be that Larson—in his pursuit of Kate's affections—read more into her words than was said.

"I've straightened it out," he said, "but it caused considerable anguish for a few days."

A smile passed quickly over his daughter's face and Jared winced.

His mother-in-law was shaking her head in disbelief. "He should've realized that ladies don't interfere in the business of gentlemen. What was that man thinking?"

"Frank Larson drove out to the farm to apologize," Jared said. "The bank has returned the loan to its original footing."

"As well he should," Mrs. Evans said. "We should put this behind us."

"Well, he's no friend of mine anymore," Kate huffed.

Jared was glad that some good had come out of this debacle.

Kate scrunched up her face, looking peeved. "That farmer woman has interfered with us too much of late. First she needed help for that tiny fire and then she wanted us to flood our meadow to save her land. Now, I'm being accused of calling her crop loan."

Jared would've preferred a more positive introduction to the subject of his engagement. He drew in a deep breath and squashed down anxiety churning in his stomach. "She'll be in our lives more often," he said. "We agreed to marry."

"You what!" his daughter screeched. The intensity of it surprised him.

"We agreed to marry."

"Never," she gasped. She stopped and turned to her father, a look of horror on her face. "My mother..."

Her grandmother took Kate's gloved hand. "My dear grandchild, my darling daughter is long gone from this world. Your father has a right to look elsewhere."

"Not with a clod," Kate sputtered. "Not...with a woman...who...lacks social graces."

"That's not for you to say." Anger built at his daughter's words. His Ida had social graces when put into circumstances that required them. Kate would come to see that when she had more exposure to his future wife.

"That's true, dear," her grandmother said. "It's not for you to say."

"Besides, you'll be choosing a husband soon," Jared said. "Your grandmother will go with you to run your household. I'll be alone. I'll need someone to supervise my house."

He noticed Mrs. Evans nodding in agreement.

"Someone from your own class," his daughter said, her voice heated, "not a farmer with so little money she needs a crop loan to get by."

Jared glared at his daughter. "We love each other."

"*Eeeek!*" Kate shrieked. "How can you say something like that?"

"Ida asked for a long engagement," Jared said, trying for a conciliatory tone. "We might even wait until you're married and in your own home."

Remembering Wednesday night, he hoped not. It was a compromise he really didn't want to make.

Tears were streaming down Kate's face. "What about Mother?"

He reached for his daughter's hand, but she jerked away. "I'll always love your mother."

"Get away from me." She turned on her heel and started running. "I don't want anything to do with you." Skirts billowing, Kate ran back toward the hotel, leaving her grandmother and her father stranded on the boardwalk, looking after her.

"I'll talk with her," his mother-in-law said with a deep sigh. "Dear Kate was devoted to her mother."

"I intend to remarry," he said. "I won't be put off by her objection."

"Keep your distance for awhile. I'll talk with her. She'll settle down."

With ladylike steps, Mrs. Evans hurried after her granddaughter, leaving Jared bereft on the sidewalk. He'd stirred things up rather than resolving issues like he'd intended when he set off for Sheridan this morning. Looking over what was said, he saw no way to reconcile his happiness with that of his daughter.

Chapter 19

Almost two weeks later, Beau Campbell grumbled to his uncle and Avilos over a whiskey in a dingy saloon on the outskirts of Buffalo. "That blasted rancher is hanging around the Osterbach woman." They had commandeered an isolated, dilapidated table out of hearing of the other patrons. Nonetheless, they kept their voices low.

Beau tilted his chair back against the wall, while he cradled his drink on his belly. The lack of movement in his takeover plans ate at him. He wished it were the good old days when he could use a gun to settle any dispute.

"Heard they was a-courtin'," Art said.

"Ganging up on me is more like it."

His uncle chuckled. "When I seen 'em together, they wasn't thinkin' about you."

Beau slammed his fist against the table, causing saloon patrons to look their way. He took off his black Stetson to run his fingers restlessly through his hair, a signal of the depth of his distress. He reined in his temper. "That woman hasn't been in the fields much since Buell has come calling. Makes it tough to do anything to her and get away clean. I need to convince her to pull up roots."

"Hit *la puta* inside the farmhouse," his friend said. "Pick a time the men are in the fields."

Beau thought about that. "You might have the right of it, my friend."

"Best be careful," his uncle said. "Them's well liked. I'm not much sure how folks have taken to you."

"I'm winning them over." Beau felt confident of this. "I'm buying significant allies."

Art finished his whiskey and put a chew of tobacco into his mouth. He packed it back along his teeth until the skin on his cheek bulged out. "Folks don't like yer friends, tho'. I heared 'em grumblin' about picked pockets and robberies."

Beau put his Stetson back on and slumped into the chair while fingering his shot glass. "The boys get restless."

"¡*Los pendejos*!" Diablo said. "I'll get 'em back in line."

"Iffen you don't watch out, nephew, you'll get caught."

"I need that creek water. I need her out of there."

"Yer puttin' the cart afore the horse," Art cautioned. "Git my place fixed first."

Beau sneered. "Your spread's worthless without that farm's water."

Art spit tobacco juice at the spittoon in the corner. "Could be bitin' off more than you kin chew. Your other stuff's risky."

"What you talking about, Old Timer?"

"Rustlin' Buell's cattle."

"I spent years rustling other men's cattle. I know what I'm doing."

"While yer was movin' on," his uncle said, "but yer stayin' in one spot now. Folks notice."

The pot was calling the kettle black. "You're a good one to lecture me. What about the meat you sell to the railroad?"

"Small potatoes," Art said. "And butchered. There ain't no brand."

Beau's face and neck turned hot as his temper flared. "I know what I'm doing, Old Man. Stay out of this."

"Only tryin' to be helpful."

"You hang your hat on my charitable nature. Get me angry and I'll find another charity."

"*Dios.* Art's only tryin' to help."

Beau glared at his friend. "By questioning my every move?"

"Don't hurt to listen," Diablo said.

"I go after what I want. What is there to learn from listening?"

"This time's different. You want to get hitched to a rich girl. You want respect."

"So?"

"Takes careful planning, *amigo*," Diablo said. "You go down and you take me with you."

"He's right, nephew. He's to run the ranch while you're livin' in town with yer family."

"I have a stake in this."

"Never fear, my faithful friend. I'll make this happen. Where there's a will there's a way and the Good Lord blessed me with a powerful will."

His uncle spat. He looked slant-eyed at his nephew and said, "Yep. Yer always bin a strong-willed son of a bitch."

Chapter 20

Five days later, Ida dropped the pan of chicken feed by the coop door and dodged bullets. Adrenalin pumped through her veins as she turned and ran flat out for the farmhouse. Her heart was beating rapidly. She'd been negligent and didn't hear the Indians ride up until almost too late. She winced when an arrow hit the solid kitchen door just as she was slamming it shut.

She'd had no time to strike the dinner bell on the back porch to alert Ernest and the hands that there was trouble. The men were repairing flood-damaged fencing near the Bar J property and were probably too far away to hear sporadic gunfire.

"What's going on," Peggy screamed.

"Renegades," Ida said as she closed the kitchen shutters.

"Oh, my God."

"If I hadn't looked up when I heard their horses at the last minute," Ida said, "they would've had me trapped in the chicken coop with no gun."

"How many are there?" Peggy brought loaded pistols to

the table and handed the shotgun and rifle to Ida before bringing more ammunition.

"I didn't stop to count," she answered between rapid breaths as she loaded the guns.

"I'll check out front to see if any are there." Peggy hurried into the hallway, taking a loaded pistol with her.

Ida cracked open a shutter on the kitchen window. "I only see one now."

The man with a folded bandana tied around his stringy, black hair and war paint obscuring his face dismounted, opened the chicken coop door and scattered the hens. The rooster ran toward him and he kicked it out of his way. He wore a faded plaid shirt and carried a bow and a quiver of arrows on his back. She wondered why he hadn't used more of them instead of the noisy rifle. A wicked-looking knife was tucked into a sheath on his belt. There was something familiar about him.

"There are two on this side," Peggy yelled from her position by the front door.

"What are they doing?"

"One's just sitting his horse. The other's looking the house over. Strange, don't you think?"

"Waiting for us to show ourselves."

"Or maybe trying to scout a way in," Peggy said.

Ida frowned. "Usually renegades hit hard and run."

"I don't like a cat and mouse game," her friend said.

"Since they opened the coop, I'd have thought they'd have stolen some chickens and left by now. Maybe they'll take one of the sheep if they're hungry enough."

"Maybe they're after guns and want to get inside," Peggy said.

Ida crossed to the other kitchen window and peeked out through the shutter, but didn't see anyone on that side of the house. "I still see only one rider," she said as she dropped the shutter and crossed the kitchen to her original position. "That's three of them."

When she looked through that shutter a moment later, she yelled, "I don't believe it!"

"Now what?"

"He's lighting the signal fire."

"Why?" Peggy sounded puzzled. "That'll only help us."

The man poked at the fire with a stick to get it to burn.

"Don't ask me, but he's getting it going pretty good."

A heavy gray smoke rose into the atmosphere. She thought about opening the window to shoot, but decided against it. It would give him plenty of warning to use that rifle in his hand. Besides, the signal fire benefited them.

A few minutes passed and Ida found out why the renegade lit the fire. He was kicking the burning wood against the clapboard house and its wooden stoop.

"He's trying to burn down the house." Ida's heart pounded. She had to act despite the danger. If she waited too long, the steps and the side of the house would catch on fire.

"I'm going out. I need to put that out."

"Wait a minute," Peggy yelled. "I've got a tub of water ready for the laundry. We can use that."

Ida heard the front door porthole slam shut. Peggy's rapid footsteps were already coming through the hallway even as she watched the renegade retreat to the protection of the water trough.

"I'll cover you," Peggy said as she entered the kitchen, puffing a little from exertion aggravated by the extra pounds put on since her husband died.

"That tub's heavy when full," Ida pointed out.

"We'll both lug it to the door," Peggy said. "Then I'll cover you while you tip it over the back steps, you see?"

When everything was ready, Ida cracked open the kitchen door. The renegade jumped to shelter behind the trough after Peggy placed a shot by his right ear. As he ducked for cover, Ida spilled the tub water over the back stoop, then dashed outside to grab the wooden mallet and give the dinner bell several good whacks. She jumped back inside, feeling vulnerable, when a bullet plowed into the now-closed, kitchen door. Blood pounded in her temples. She much preferred farming to fighting.

The two men from the front of the house rode up to help their friend. They leapt from their horses and sheltered behind the bunkhouse.

Peggy plopped into a kitchen chair. "We're stuck inside here with three of them out there waiting to shoot us."

"I wonder how long it will take our men to return from the fields." Anxiety building, Ida peered through the kitchen shutters. "There are fires still going."

"I'll refill the tub." Peggy grabbed its metal handles and carried it across the kitchen to the sink.

"That'll take too long. What if I shot holes in the rainwater barrel? It would spill along the side of the house."

"Might work, I guess. Just in case, I'll keep pumping."

Ida opened the side kitchen window away from the view of the Indians and shot two holes low down on the barrel so it would flood the ground along the house's foundation. It was satisfying to see the water pouring out of the barrel before she drew her head back inside.

Within seconds, Ida heard scattered shots and thundering hooves. "Now what?"

"Wouldn't you know it, more Indians," Peggy said as she peered out through the shutters. "They're blocked by the barn now. I can't count how many."

Ida groaned. There was only so much they could hold off. If the Indians tried flaming arrows or blocked the chimney, they'd smoke her and Peggy out. She prayed their men would get here before then.

A shrill whistle sounded. Peggy—still looking through the shutters—said, "Those first three have whistled for their horses, can you believe it?"

"Maybe they're going to ride out to the others."

"Not so. They're no friends of these three, are they?" Peggy grinned. "They're taking off."

Ida peered through the kitchen shutters and saw the outlaws mounting their horses and riding away. "I'll check out front." She grabbed a pistol from the table and ran into the hallway.

"And I know why," Peggy yelled after her. "It's Chief Long Wolf and his friends on their tails." After a few minutes, she added, "Looks like Mr. Buell is with them."

Ida's heart leapt. She watched with relief from the front portal as the renegades galloped off.

Peggy burst out laughing. "Those cowards are riding

hell for leather out of here, with the Sioux whooping and hollering right behind them."

Drained, Ida sagged against the front door. All her nerve endings jangled.

"What do you think about some warmed milk to settle us down?" Peggy said from the kitchen.

"Good thinking. I'm shaking like a bowl of pudding."

She watched Jared rein in his horse as the Wild West Indians roared past the front of the farmhouse. He tied the reins to the railing and took the porch steps two at a time. He was looking extremely handsome in his banker's clothes.

Ida was suddenly aware that strands of hair had come loose from her braid and stuck out awkwardly. She patted at her hair while she looked down at clothing still carrying the dust from spilled chicken feed. She wished she looked better. "Can't be helped," she muttered to herself as she opened the door. Ida wanted to kiss Jared soundly. Instead, she invited him in for coffee.

"Are you all right?" He stepped over the threshold.

"Shaken." She made her unsteady way from the front door to the kitchen. "Were you traveling with Long Wolf?"

"When I got closer, I met up with him," Jared said, "but I'd heard shots and saw the smoke while on my way to town. I detoured to check it out."

"We thought you were more renegades," she said. "We heard your horses, but couldn't see you because of the barn."

"I'm sorry." He must have recognized the strain in her voice because he apologized.

She led him to the kitchen and Peggy got him settled in with a cup of coffee and a buttered biscuit. Ida opened the kitchen shutters and the back door to the late morning sunlight. She excused herself to go outside. She stepped out the kitchen door, anxious to make sure the fires were out and to discover what happened to the scattered chickens.

Jared rose to come with her. She stopped him.

"Stay there. No need to get all dirty. If I need help, I'll call."

He nodded and reached for another of the biscuits set out on a metal platter.

It didn't take long for Ida to see that the remnants of the soggy fire were well out. The chickens had returned to the hen house and were busy clucking and pecking at the spilled feed. Content there would likely be no interruption in the laying of eggs because the hens had settled down, Ida returned to the kitchen. Her warmed milk sat cooling at her place at the table. Peggy was already sipping hers and giving Jared an accounting of the morning's events.

"You two are resourceful," he said with respect in his voice.

Ten minutes later, after coffee, warm milk and some polite conversation, Ida heard horses' hooves on the roadway. The Sioux had returned. She and Jared went to the front door to invite them in. Peggy called out to offer the Indians coffee and biscuits.

"We saw your signal," Long Wolf said as the chiefs settled themselves at the kitchen table. Ida didn't correct his misperception to tell him the renegades had started the fire.

"You know," Peggy said, "I didn't think there was enough smoke before they forced us to douse it."

"Eyes good. Spot smoke," Chief Flies Above said.

"They tried to burn us out." Ida looked around the table at the men. She was grateful that today she and Peggy didn't need to go it alone. Years past, she'd have gritted her teeth and done it all herself. These days she expected—and valued—help offered by friends.

"You're not injured?" Chief Long Wolf asked.

"We barricaded ourselves in before the renegades could get to us."

"No Indians," Chief Flies Above said curtly.

"They weren't?"

"Horses shod. Bow carried wrong way. White men dress up to burn you out," Flies Above said, "and blame us."

"We chased them back to the Campbell ranch property line," Chief Long Wolf said around a bite of biscuit.

The Campbells again.

"Scared them good," Flies Above said. "Maybe they'll think twice before they step on your land."

Ida certainly hoped so.

A noise made her look out the opened kitchen door. Ernest and the two field hands were walking tiredly across the barnyard. They must have realized the emergency was over because they weren't hurrying.

Hank was the first to step into the kitchen. "Hey, we got company." He spoke for the benefit of the two men behind him. "Was the signal fire for you?" he asked, acknowledging the chiefs seated at the table. "It got a little out of hand, didn't it?"

Ernest entered the doorway, asking, "What did I miss?" He hung his wide-brimmed hat on a wall hook and rinsed off farm dirt at the kitchen pump before shaking hands with their guests.

"What's cooking?" Buck said when he entered through the doorway a moment later. "I can't smell a single, solitary thing because of that soggy mess outside."

"Cooking?" Peggy's voice was questioning.

"Yeah," Buck said. "You rang the dinner bell."

Ida and Peggy looked at each other and burst out laughing. The men hadn't responded to an emergency because they thought the bell called them to their mid-day meal. Ida would have to work out a way to show the difference before another emergency arose.

"I haven't started the meal." Peggy bent elbows to hoist herself up from the table. She headed for the pantry. "We've had some excitement around here, haven't we?"

The laughter had broken Ida's tension. Her world was coming back into place. "That wasn't the dinner bell. That was the emergency bell."

"It was providential, wasn't it," Peggy said, looking at Ida, "that the Chiefs and Mr. Buell came along. We would still be holed up inside here. And you men might have walked into their trap."

She shooed the field hands out of her way. "You go outside to wash up. I need to get at that end of the table if I'm to get your meal on."

"We'll tell you everything while you eat," Ida said.

Jared excused himself so he could travel to his meeting in town.

"I'll see you out," Ida offered.

"I can find my own way," he said. "Stay and tell your cousin what happened this morning."

She stared longingly at Jared's back until he disappeared into the darkened hallway. She heard the front door open and close, then turned to Ernest when Hank and Buck re-entered the kitchen.

"Sit down, cousin, and I'll tell you all about it."

Chapter 21

Before dusk Monday evening, Ida was resting on the front porch rocking chair after dinner when Jared rode up to the farmhouse at a fairly good clip. As soon as she recognized him, she released her grip on the pistol in her pocket. Unobtrusively, she fingered the buttons on her faded house dress to make sure she was decent. She'd unbuttoned a few to let the cooler evening air in. A slight wind ruffled the lace collar at her neck.

Jared dismounted, hitched his horse to the rail, walked with long strides toward her and mounted the steps two at a time. She thought he looked stressed and tired. His attire showed hard use from the trails. Sweat and dust coated both shirt and pants. After a distracted peck on her cheek, he slumped down on the top step, his back resting against the porch post.

"You look troubled. What's up?"

He looked up at her. "I'm making battle plans."

"Battle…"

Jared nodded, looking solemn. "We can't wait around. We need to act."

"Why now?"

You and Peggy were attacked Friday. I lost cattle again last night."

"No!"

"We tracked the thieves most of the day, but no luck. They herded my cattle onto well-used paths so we could no longer see their sign."

He wiped a hand across his brow as if to clear away a troublesome burden. "The rustlers keep getting away. I've posted extra guards and moved cattle farther out." Frustration coated his words.

"Maybe they won't find them in the outer ranges."

"And I've hired some new men who can handle a gun."

She inhaled sharply. Images from the Johnson County range wars flew into her head.

"Waiting's too risky," he said. "I should force Campbell to back down."

Her heart contracted when she noticed he used "I" and didn't include her, but she decided to let it slide for now. "What about the peace officers? Where are they?"

"The marshal telegraphed," Jared said. "He's tied up in Laramie in trials. Sheriff Angus is still out of town and no one knows when he'll be back."

"Troublesome."

"Deputy Trainer can keep a sharp eye on a peaceful town, but he's just about useless when it comes to a confrontation where guns are likely. I'm pretty much on my own."

Her heart dropped to her stomach. He'd done it again. He'd left her out.

"Right now he's being inconspicuous," he said. "He's letting his cohorts do the dirty work.

"Wise on his part."

"Calling him out on rustling might make him get careless."

She nodded. "Bring him out of the shadows."

Jared leaned over the wooden porch floor and massaged the toe of a shoe that peeked from beneath her skirts. The intimacy of his touch on her toes through the soft kid leather caused a blush.

"People need to see him for what he is." Jared momentarily distracted her from her toes. "Right now he's hoodwinked a good many folks. They need to hear what he's been doing to force you to sell." He looked up at her. "You're in too much danger here. Move to the ranch so I can take care of you."

"Abandon Ernest and Peggy?" It was unthinkable.

"Only for a little while."

"What would your daughter say?" She had a pretty good idea of what the daughter would say.

"She's in Sheridan with her grandmother. They'll stay there until this clash with Campbell is over."

Ida rocked forward and planted her feet solidly on the floorboards. She really didn't have to think about his proposal. "Thanks, but no thanks. I'll stay on the farm." Her tone squashed any dissent. She crossed over to the narrow porch bench, sat at one end and patted a spot on the bench next to her. "Sit here. I'll massage that tension out of your shoulders."

Jared unfolded his long frame from the porch steps,

walked over and straddled the bench. An odor of sweat and dust clung to him.

Ida massaged his shoulders through a layer of sweat-stained cotton twill.

"He won't stop," Jared said, "until he's cleared everything and everybody out of his way."

"I won't budge," she said.

"That's the problem." His voice sounded pained.

"What about you? I don't want anything to happen to you." The thought of him injured caused gall to rise. She'd lost one man to a bullet. She couldn't lose another.

The sounds of tree toads and other night creatures hovered on the edges of her awareness as she wrestled with her thoughts. She had no choice. She must defend her property. They needed allies when they talked with Beau. "We'll need friends with us."

"What's with 'us'?" Jared asked.

She ignored the question. "Prominent citizens of the kind Campbell wants to impress. He won't make a scene when we talk with him if it's in front of the social elite."

"What's with this 'we'?"

"I don't like fighting," she said, ignoring him again, "but Beau Campbell has sweet-talked, threatened, tried arson, attacked my wagon, shot Todd and sent gunmen to the farmhouse. I can't be shut out."

"You need to protect yourself," he said.

"I need to be a part of this. I know people in town who'll help."

"We'll need good people—men who won't panic if guns come out during negotiations."

Tension fled when she realized he'd acceded. "I know some."

"Like the men who fought the Texans?" Jared asked. "They're seasoned."

"Yes." Ida harked back to the uncertain times of the range war. Would they be starting another such battle? Unease lay upon her. "I want Beau to stop. If this is the way to stop him, I'll do it."

Jared placed lean hands on her shoulders. "Can you ride to Buffalo with me tomorrow?"

"I can get away." She didn't even take the time to think about the disruption to the farm chores. She'd do what needed to be done.

"I'll bring a horse so Ernest can work Old Molly," he said.

"I'd be grateful."

"Can you leave just after dawn?"

"Of course. I'll get the animals fed before I leave."

While the still of night descended, they sat head-to-head on the bench planning the trip. After a while, they took a walk down by the willow tree.

* * * *

The blanket of stars seemed brighter when Jared rode homeward across the darkened meadowland that evening. A few short months ago he'd thought Ida untutored and gauche. Since then, he'd learned she possessed a gracefulness and intelligence hidden by the harsh reality of farm labor. As a youth in Illinois, she'd acquired schooling in bookkeeping, grammar, geography, science and math, a little Latin and a foundation in literature—beyond that normally provided a girl. She loved classical music and skillfully played the harp and the piano.

While the stallion slowly trotted across the darkened landscape, Jared found himself whistling—something he hadn't done since his courtship of Isabella.

Chapter 22

"You're pushin' yer luck," Beau Campbell's uncle said in the dark hours before dawn. He and Art were eating an early breakfast at the battered kitchen table. The blue-enameled coffeepot noisily perked on the wood-burning stove. Flapjacks dripped with butter and honey.

"Too many fights in town by those so-called friends of yourn. It'll turn the good citizens against you," Art said, "if it hasn't already."

Beau shrugged, tossing off his uncle's protest.

"The boys need a little recreational fun. They get bored cooped up in that dilapidated shed you call a bunkhouse."

His uncle took a moment to hawk up phlegm. "Them'll be more bored sittin' in a jail cell." Art waved the flapjack flipper at his nephew to emphasize his point. "I tell you, nephew, I've lived 'ere a long time. These people ain't gonna put up with yer shenanigans."

Beau guffawed. Specks of half-chewed food spit in all directions. He wiped his mouth on his sleeve.

"The bastard sheriff's out of town and the deputy's a pussy cat. They're helpless."

"Don't be too sure. Them men survived Indians. They'll start comin' after you if you don't watch out."

"Just let them try."

* * * *

Before dawn, while putting breakfast on the table, Peggy teased her mercilessly. She hinted at an elopement because, unexpectedly, Ida's beau was taking her to town. Peggy knew the true reason for the trip into Buffalo. She used her joking as a way to mask concern. Ida pretended to be upset.

She was wearing serviceable breeches and a long-sleeved blouse of a better quality than she wore to the fields. A skirt and a petticoat were packed in her saddle bags. When she got to town, she'd change at Martha's place. Her high-heeled boots would suffice both for riding and for walking the planked sidewalks in Buffalo.

She was of two minds about this trip. There was no way she wanted to stand up to Campbell's wrath on their own. They needed the town behind them. On the other hand, she'd be more than grateful if the good Lord made everything go away so she could concentrate on farming and getting to know Jared better. Still, Ida knew she was a woman who faced each day's challenges and shirked none. She'd carry out her part come hell or high water.

She went over everything packed in the saddlebags and double-checked all of the day's arrangements with Ernest. While checking off the list, Ida remembered how often in the past she'd worried about being away and had given up town pleasures to keep the farm under her watchful eye. Today, she was content to leave the farm in her cousin's capable hands. Almost losing everything to a flood—including themselves—had radically changed her priorities. She now easily shared her responsibilities with those who'd helped her survive.

Jared arrived, trailing a dappled gray gelding. Before Ida mounted, she slung the packed saddle bags onto the gelding, slipped her rifle into the leather sheath and dropped a pistol and ammunition into her handbag.

* * * *

"This is a new experience for me," she told Jared, "going to town on a work day."

"I'm there a lot during the week because of bank business."

"I seldom go." She urged the gelding to a trot alongside Jared's mount. "I get so tired that I stay close to home where I can rest."

"I can understand that."

"After Dean was murdered, I worried something would happen at the farm if I was away. Scuffling with Campbell has made me realize how well my cousin and Peggy and the farm hands back me up. I don't worry so much."

The air was crisp and had a bite to it when the wind picked up. Behind nearby bushes and rocks, birds and small animals noisily fled as they passed. Ida's eyes calculated the amount of water remaining on the snow-capped Big Horn Mountains bordering their passage toward Buffalo. Her crops would need every drop by late summer, but they didn't need more of it now. Her land was still drying out.

As they rode, they determined who should be in on the

planning for the confrontation with Beau. Ida was surprised by how many of the same people they both knew. She laughed.

"Our acquaintances must've been extra careful not to invite us to entertainments on the same day."

Jared laughed heartily. "They must have made sure we didn't bump into each other."

"They're probably bewildered that we're engaged."

"They'll get over it."

"How many do you think will join us?"

"Doesn't matter. We need to do something. We can't sit around and wait for Beau to take over."

* * * *

As Ida rode into Buffalo on her first trip to town since the flood, she marveled at the debris from sheds and out-houses from other sections of town that had floated against Clear Creek Bridge. The debris still partially blocked the flow of water. Unfortunately for the citizenry, the drugstore was a complete loss. She'd have to find out where they'd relocated and if some of the remedies they needed on the farm survived the waters. She was running low on liniment for Old Molly's legs.

The Occidental Hotel had lost one whole section in back, but not anything to require a closure for business. Most of the remaining Main Street buildings, including her friends' store, had minimal damage.

After stabling their horses at the livery barn, Ida changed into her skirt at Martha's home. The pastor had offered the church hall for their afternoon meeting. They stopped at the jail to let the deputy sheriff know what they planned. Then they visited their Buffalo friends to invite them to the meeting.

As they visited from house to house, they discovered their courtship was well known. They found themselves fending off questions about the wedding date. By the time Ida and Jared arrived at the church hall after a mid-day meal at the Occidental, a full three dozen people were assembled—friends having brought friends of their own.

After shaking hands all around and thanking everyone for attending on short notice, she and Jared mounted the stage. Ida found she had butterflies in her stomach as they took turns explaining the various attacks at the farm and the rustling at the ranch.

"We can't wait for the sheriff to return," Jared said. "Campbell must learn that we're keeping an eye on him and his cohorts and that they'd better mend their ways."

"That's why we need your help." Ida concluded her story to what looked like a stunned audience.

A nagging doubt plagued her. Beau had gone out of his way to make friends in town. His sweet-talking tongue could convince folks to trust him—until you got to know the other side of him, that is. Would these people leave Jared and her to struggle alone against a Campbell gang steadily increasing in size? Or would they stand with them, shoulder to shoulder?

"Let me make sure I understand this, Jared." The banker, Larson, rose to his feet. "You sent your daughter and mother-in-law to Sheridan because you believe Beau Campbell is getting increasingly violent."

"I did and I do."

"May I remind you that he is a major depositor at the bank?" Larson glared at Jared. "Campbell acts decently in town. Why, I myself have had some interesting conversations with the man. It's his wranglers who get into trouble."

Jared explained about the Kansas killings and his telegrams to start the Pinkerton investigation. "I know him. Eventually he'll try to take over the town. We have to stop him now."

"You acknowledged it's been a dozen years since the Kansas incident," Larson said. "People change. He may have nothing to do with these recent attacks."

"I saw him," Ida broke in, even though Larson was ignoring her and speaking directly to Jared. "His friend is the one who shot at Ernest and me while we were planting. Campbell stayed in the background."

"A stray shot while hunting rabbits."

"What decent man would shoot at game in our direct path and then raise the gun in defiance? Besides, if they carelessly shot near me, they'd shoot at any woman."

Larson settled back into his seat. "I'm glad Miss Buell is in Sheridan. I wouldn't want her to be frightened."

"There have been enough incidents to warrant action," Jared said.

Heads nodded in side conversations and feet shuffled as they absorbed the significance of what they'd just heard. When the mumblings died down, one large woman in a brightly flowered dress spoke up. "There've been a lot of roughnecks in town of late."

"I had my pocket picked the other night in the saloon," a wiry man in a fringed leather vest said. "The only one close by was one of them new Campbell riders."

Others affirmed an increase in the number of things lifted from store shelves.

"I've been missing a few cattle most weeks since Campbell arrived," Jared said. "We lose the trail, but it heads out toward the Badlands. Some say Beau's newly hired riders are from there."

"The Robinson house was robbed last week," a woman said. "Buffalo hasn't had anything like that for years."

After comparing notes—and to Ida's relief—the townsfolk decided there were too many incidences of theft and increasing violence since Beau came to town. They'd make their position clear that it had to stop.

The men went off to a corner of the room to make war plans. The women were settling down to chat and await their men folk. A flood of relief that she and Jared had the support of Buffalo's most powerful citizens swept through Ida. As she crossed the room to join the men in the planning group, she mentally seconded the conclusions of the heavyset woman she overheard saying, "Beau Campbell's charming Southern manners never fooled me."

Chapter 23

Twenty minutes from her farmhouse—homeward bound after the Buffalo meeting—a bullet whizzed past Ida's head and ricocheted off a nearby rock. She and Jared leapt from their horses to crouch behind boulders by a roadside ditch. Their mounts took off down the road when two more shots slammed into the dirt near their hooves.

Not again, she thought.

Her heart beat erratically as she tried to figure out what was happening. Fingers of fear spread between her shoulder blades when she spotted two riders coming from the direction of the Campbell ranch.

Beau again.

The men dismounted and sent another bullet their way before disappearing behind boulders on the other side of the roadway. She glanced at Jared who was just inches away and saw worry lines on his face.

She'd instinctively grabbed the rifle from its sheath as she jumped from the gelding. Squatting beside Jared, she checked to see that it was loaded and cocked. To be sure her pistol was still there, she patted its bulge in the bag tied to the leather belt holding up her breeches.

"How did Beau know we were in Buffalo?" she whispered. "We just decided on the meeting last night."

"Word of mouth travels fast."

"We were careless. It could've gotten us killed." She spoke quietly so her voice wouldn't carry.

"They've got our attention now," he said.

"They're behind those rocks where that bush is growing."

"Do you have a shot?"

"No."

"We'll have to wait them out."

He motioned that he'd keep an eye out to the left and straight ahead. Ida should cover the right side and the rear. She checked for escape routes to use if they were rushed while she willed her tense shoulders to relax and made herself as comfortable as possible against the rock's face. If she needed to move quickly, it would be unwise to have pins and needles.

Even though Jared was a man she could trust in a fight, she felt uneasy. Defending herself with a gun was not her idea of fun.

"My rifle's on my horse." Jared whistled and his mount's ears went up. The horse trotted towards them from where it had stopped farther down the road. The dappled gray followed.

Jared quickly retrieved his rifle from its sheath. Although he was protected by his mount, another bullet ricocheted threateningly off the rocks. He dropped to shelter after slapping the horse on its rear to send it back up the road.

Ida's mount trotted after it. She wished—while her horse was near—she'd thought to grab the food Martha stowed in her saddlebag. It was the supper hour and there was no telling how much longer they would be trapped.

"In a couple of hours it'll get dark," Jared said. "We'll be able to slip away."

She strained her ears, but all was quiet. Not even a bird chirped. "Do you think they're sneaking up?" she whispered.

"I'll see if they're still near that bush." Jared removed his Stetson and raised it above the rim of the boulder. A shot rang out and the hat tumbled to the dry earth. Ida fired her rifle as soon as the shooter became exposed. She heard a yelp of pain.

"Got him." Jared sounded pleased. "Good for you."

She was pleased he recognized her ability, although it wasn't her best. "I probably just grazed him. It happened too fast for a good shot."

"It'll slow him down."

"I didn't see the second man," she whispered. "Where did he get to?"

He hunched his shoulders. "I'm going to shake them up a bit. See if the second man will shoot back."

"How?"

"They won't fall for the hat trick again and I've got nothing else I want to sacrifice."

"There's nothing I want you to sacrifice either." She'd finally found someone as important to her as Dean. She didn't want a hole in him.

He fired a few shots randomly near the boulders. There

was no return fire, only sounds of mumbling.

"Why didn't they shoot back?" she asked, puzzled.

Jared shrugged.

The gunmen were talking again and Ida wished she could make out what they were saying. She crouched closer to the edge of the boulder to listen. Being a woman of action, she found waiting exhausting. Impatience entwined itself around her gut, increasing tenseness. "I wish they'd get on with it," she said, testily. "I'm not a patient woman."

Jared laughed. It burst out in a fulsome baritone. His strong back shook, but his rifle remained firmly under control. "Shall I tell them to start firing so you have something to do?" he asked around a gulp of air.

"No wisecracks." She slapped his upper arm, but she couldn't help adding a grin. This was certainly the strangest gun battle she'd ever been in.

A commotion caused by the scraping of feet and jiggling of spurs drew her attention.

Jared held up a hand and twisted his head to listen. "They seem to be obliging you."

A man burst from behind the rock. The other shooter lay down covering fire. Jared squeezed off a shot, but there was no accompanying cry of pain. "Damn. I missed."

Jared's disgruntled look made her throw back her head and chuckle.

"Laugh at me, will you? We'll see who gets the last laugh." He reached over and pulled out a hair pin so that her braid loosened. He brushed the back of his hand lightly over her cheek, down her shoulder and along the curve of her breast. Her blood suddenly heated.

Jared seemed to have no problem keeping his eye on the enemy while stroking her. For Ida, concentration was proving difficult.

The shooter returned, riding swiftly behind boulders on his side of the road and towing a horse. Jared leaned forward and peered out to see what the men were doing.

Ida caught sounds of movement. They were mounting their horses to charge. "Here they come." Her stomach clenched as she prepared for the attack. But she was wrong. The men weren't rushing them. To her astonishment, they beat a hasty retreat toward Campbell land. She listened to the pounding hooves until there was nothing more to hear.

"They're gone," she said, but she kept her rifle within easy reach. In the shelter of the boulders, she stretched the kinks out of her back. Pent-up tension slowly drained away.

"I don't want you to leave this ditch, Ida, only to find someone else out there." Jared circled around the rock face. "I'll check it out."

Much of the strain had left his face. A few minutes later he called from the opposite side of the road, "They're gone."

"That's a blessing."

Jared trotted across the roadway, whistling to his horse. The mount's head went up and its ears moved back and forth. At another whistle, it started in their direction. Her horse followed, carrying the saddle bag with Martha's picnic supper.

"Do you mind if we take the time to eat?" Ida felt somewhat ridiculous that the first thing to catch her attention after a gun fight was her empty stomach.

Jared studied her, his hand under her chin. "You look

like you could use something solid in your stomach. The ranch and the farm can wait."

"Bless you," she said.

"I have a blanket in my saddle bag to sit on." He cleared a patch of earth of pebbles and debris.

"We can roll my town clothes and use them for pillows," she said.

Snagging the bridle of Jared's horse, Ida maneuvered the animal close and retrieved a wool blanket patterned in a brightly colored Indian design. She spread it at the base of the boulder on the patch of earth Jared had cleared.

Pushing his stallion out of the way, she snagged her horse's bridle and positioned the mount so the leather saddle bags were easily accessible. Rummaging around inside the bags, she dug out her skirt and petticoat. Dropping them onto the blanket, she rummaged some more and hauled out the food sack Martha had packed. She slapped the gelding on its rear and both horses took off down the road. They eventually stopped and wandered in search of their own supper.

She crouched down onto the blanket and opened the draw string of Martha's cloth sack. When she looked inside, she found boiled eggs and apples and pieces of fried chicken wrapped in a kitchen towel. She spread the food out on the blanket.

"Want a leg or a breast?"

"A leg."

She gave Jared a chicken leg and sat down on the blanket to eat hers. The wadded skirt and petticoat were wedged behind her as cushioning against the boulder's hardness. As the first bites slid toward her growling stomach, she said, "So much better."

Jared joined her on the blanket. The smells of dust and saddle soap and horse hair clung to him. He chose an egg and an apple to round out his supper. Where his hip met hers, warmth spread into her belly.

Dusk was coming. The land darkened around them as they ate. When finished, Ida stood and stretched. "I'd best get home before Peggy starts worrying." She was bending over to re-pack the left-overs when Jared's hand captured the calf of her leg and pulled her back down onto the blanket.

"Stay a little longer." The timbre of his voice forewarned her. Her breath caught at his eagerness.

In short order, she found herself pressed against a hard chest. The metal buttons of his plaid shirt cut into her cheek. It didn't matter. Her ear was drawn to the pounding of his heart, which drowned out the sounds of Nature. She shivered when he ran lean fingers over the sensitized skin at her neckline and roamed toward her cleavage. Jared unhooked her belt. The pouch where she had stored her pistol thumped to the earth.

She unbuttoned her shirt and trembled as he brushed aside the camisole. Cooled evening air caressed her bared flesh. His fingertips languidly charted breast and nipple. With sure fingers, he undid her trouser buttons and pushed aside the confining garment.

Ida tugged Jared's shirttail loose and slipped her hand beneath his undershirt. Tracing each rib, she worked her hands downward. As if from a distance, she heard his groan. She lost herself in the depths of his hunger and invited his tongue to explore the moist recesses of her mouth.

She was stretched along the length of him, when, holding her tightly, he rolled over to the flat of his back. She unbuttoned Jared's trousers and pushed them away. As his manhood swelled, the difficulty in her breathing increased exponentially. The only relief was to draw him into her.

"Now," she shouted.

* * * *

Jared was disoriented, exhausted—and thankful.

Time slowly ticked away while his sweating body and befuddled mind readjusted. He stroked the smooth skin on Ida's buttocks even as the last tremors worked through her body. He felt himself recede and he wished he had the stamina to oblige her once again. Her long braid had come loose and fallen by his ear. He took the end of it and brushed it lovingly against her cheek. She nibbled at the hand holding it.

When Ida rolled off onto her back, she unashamedly exposed her breasts and her groin to his gaze. She stood and pulled up her breeches which had ended up down around her ankles.

"You're beautiful." He meant that sincerely.

Ida dipped a curtsey with her breeches partially undone. "Thank you, kind sir."

Her beauty was that of Nature rather than Isabella's hothouse-plant beauty. Jared couldn't let this woman slip through his fingers. "We must set a wedding date." He wanted marriage—now. He wanted the sure knowledge that she'd be waiting when he came home from a long day's work.

Ida pulled her camisole into place and re-buttoned her

shirt. "For me, after the harvest is best." Her practical response to something so critical to his wellbeing evoked a flare of irritation. He forced it back down while buttoning up. "It'll be hard to wait that long."

Ida frowned. "We have problems to work out—family to consider. Neither one of us is ready to give up our homesteads."

"A woman moves with her man." Jared felt secure in that knowledge. "It's the way things are."

"I did that for Dean," Ida said. "I left my Illinois family and friends and moved to Wyoming. Being uprooted was hard. I'm not willing to be uprooted again by giving up the farm. I've put too much of myself into it." She paused before she added, "We'll have to find a compromise that includes my keeping and working my farm."

Jared's dander rose. "What kind of marriage would that be—you living at the farm and me at the ranch?"

"Sometimes you'll stay at the farm with me. Sometimes I'll stay at the ranch with you."

"As if we're migrants?"

That she sounded so practical and reasonable made his irritation grow. It would be true that sometimes cattle drives would take him away for months. She might want to move back to the farm rather than stay near Kate and his mother-in-law. But as long as he was there to protect her from their barbs, she should be at his side. "Let Ernest run the farm. I need you at the ranch to be my hostess." He needed her in his arms at night.

"Maybe later, but not right away." She shook her head. "We need to work things out."

She calmly repacked the saddle bags, seemingly unaware of the emotions churning inside of him. He opened his mouth to say something more, changed his mind and shut it firmly. Obviously, he'd need time to convince her into his way of thinking.

* * * *

Beau and the two men he'd sent after Jared and that ornery female were sprawled about the Campbell ranch bunkhouse. The air was heavy with the smells of sweat and dirty clothing. "Joe was losin' too much blood, boss," Carson explained. "He git hit early. We couldn't rush 'em."

Beau had planned an ambush that should've looked like a robbery gone bad. Instead of both being dead, the rancher and the farmer were unhurt. It was a bitter pill to swallow. He just hoped to God the men weren't recognized and traced back to him.

"Them's both good shots." Joe was lying on his bunk, his leg bandaged. "And they ain't afeared."

"That's right." Carson agreed with Joe. "Wasn't nothin' we could do. They even laughed at us."

Beau swore a blue streak. He'd have to find another way to get at that woman.

* * * *

Darkness had a firm grip on the land by the time Ida and Jared reached the cut off to the farm lane. Neither one had said much since their spat. The homestead appeared to be half-asleep. Lanterns in the kitchen and the bunkhouse created feeble veins of light that pushed at the shadows. She breathed deeply, relishing the aromas of livestock and fecund earth. This land was hers. How could she abandon it?

She wished she could change her mind for Jared's sake, but she couldn't. Each time she saw herself stepping over the ranch house threshold, she envisioned the daughter's cold distain slapping her. She'd never have a moment of peace until either Kate was gone from the house or she was converted to Ida's side. With a strong a personality like Kate's, a conversion seemed unlikely.

When they clattered into the barnyard, Ernest stepped out of the bunkhouse. He was adjusting his suspenders as if recently pulling on his pants after being aroused from slumber.

"I've been worried about you." He rubbed his eyes. She heard the concern in his voice.

"I'm so sorry. We had another Campbell incident," she said as she dismounted. She wasn't mentioning the time taken for making love.

"What was it this time?"

"Two masked men," Jared said, "acting like robbers."

"We aren't hurt," Ida hastened to assure Ernest. "I winged one of them and they took off."

"That's my cousin," he said with a grin. "Annie would be proud of her pupil."

"I was, too." Jared's praise was a pleasant surprise after his homeward bound, stony silence.

When she started unbuckling her saddle bags, Ernest asked, "Need some help?"

"They're not heavy," she said.

"How did the meeting go?"

Jared was almost finished explaining about talking with the deputy sheriff, the pastor and the town's leading citizens at the church hall when Peggy interrupted his narration. She stuck her head out the kitchen doorway. "Ida Louise Osterbach, you march yourself in here, my good friend, and tell me why you've been gone so long. I was getting ready to send out a search party, wasn't I?"

"In a minute, Peggy," she said. "I'll just say my good-byes to Jared."

That must have satisfied her. Peggy ducked back inside and Ida soon heard metal clanking at the kitchen stove. It sounded like her friend was checking the coffee pot. She must have been satisfied with the amount of coffee left because the next thing Ida heard were the coffee mugs being put out on the table.

Jared finished the run down of the meeting for Ernest and briefly told of the attack on their way home. When he was done, Ida untied the gelding from the hitching post and handed the reins to her fiancée. "Thank you for the use of the horse."

"Think about what I've had to say." Jared touched the brim of his hat, ran his heels along the sides of his horse and rode away with the gelding trotting alongside.

"What did he mean by 'think about'?" Ernest asked.

"He wants to get married right away. He doesn't want to wait."

"You should," her cousin said. "Until harvest time, we can make it without you."

Ida was not comforted by the idea that she wasn't need-ed.

Ernest decided to go back to bed rather than come into the kitchen for coffee. "Dawn comes early around here. I need my sleep." He left her, standing by the water trough, watching until Jared and the rider-less gelding disappeared into the darkness.

Ida picked up the saddlebags she'd removed from the borrowed mount and carried them into the dimly lit barn. She removed their contents, put the items into an empty flour sack and hung the saddlebags on a hook in the tack room. Slinging the cotton sack over one shoulder, she dragged herself into the kitchen and dropped the sack onto the kitchen sideboard.

"You look like something the cat dragged in." Peggy was at the kitchen sink and up to her elbows in soap suds.

"I *feel* like something the cat dragged in."

Ida started sorting out the things in the sack to put them away when Peggy waved a drippy hand at her. "They can wait a few minutes, can't they? Sit down and rest yourself. I've got the coffee out. Let me finish washing this pot and then I'll sit with you."

Ida realized she was extremely tired. It was as if all her insides were reamed out and nothing replaced them. She looked back at the flour sack and decided Peggy was right. These things could be put away in the morning.

"I want to hear all about it, don't I?" Peggy was saying. "How did that meeting go?"

Ida pulled out a chair, stretched her arms high over her head, released a yawn and sat down. The tensions of the day were easing. Weariness was seeping in.

"It's hard to know where to begin," she said, furrowing her brow.

"Begin at the beginning."

Ida shook her shoulders out and started relating the adventures of the day. She yawned. Her story might end up short if she fell asleep while telling it.

With the help of strong coffee, she managed to hit all the high points. In concluding, she said, "We have a dozen solid citizens behind us. The other two-thirds range from lukewarm to being supportive—maybe helpful if health and other reasons aren't in the way at the time we act."

"That sounds good, doesn't it?"

Ida agreed and started on the second part of her story. "Two masked gunmen attacked us about a half hour from here."

"Merciful heavens!" Peggy said. "You know, I thought I heard gunfire earlier tonight. I couldn't place where it was coming from before it stopped."

"From us. Defending ourselves."

"Oh, my dearest." Peggy came toward Ida, wiping her hands on a towel. She wrapped an arm around Ida's shoulders and gave a hug before flopping into the kitchen chair nearest her coffee mug.

"Neither one of us was hit. I nicked one of them. Soon after that they took off."

"Did you chase after them?" Peggy asked.

"Saw no need to. We could see they were riding toward the Campbell ranch. There was no use tackling them in the dark. Pretty soon that gang will be reined in by the respectable citizens of Buffalo."

"Thanks to the work you two did today."

"Amen to that."

Ida was reluctant to bring up the next part of her even-

the social hostess Jared wanted? She didn't know if she could. If she sacrificed to the point where she never planted another seed, might the sacrifice sour her and, eventually, destroy love? Would her unwillingness to commit until compromises were in place make Jared reconsider marriage?

Common sense and logical planning had been tenets by which Ida had survived many tribulations. These past two years, the farm had been her sole reason for staying in Wyoming. In her heart of hearts, she knew she couldn't easily walk away.

Jared rode swiftly into the barnyard and executed a running dismount. He loosely hitched the sweating horse to the water trough, took her damp hand and kissed it. Her heart increased its beat. Even in a dusty plaid shirt and work pants, he looked delicious.

"Are you all right?" he asked.

"Now that I see you, I'm wonderful."

Doubts faded. Somehow, she'd find a way to marry this man—and soon. She kissed him boldly on the mouth, even though there was still enough daylight for them to be seen. He wasn't smiling—like she was—when her lips left his. Instead, he looked deadly serious.

"I don't have much time," he said tersely. "I detoured from the others to let you know that we're on our way to the Campbell ranch for a showdown."

Her heart shriveled. "So soon?"

"More cattle were rustled last night. We're not waiting on the Pinkertons. We're laying down the law to Beau."

"Now?"

"We're telling him to his face: No more rustling. No

more attacks against you. No more brawling in town. No more thievery. We've had it."

"Now?"

"Might as well. We have the backing of most of the town."

Her throat tightened with tension and her heart stepped up its pounding. "I wasn't prepared for it to be so soon."

"We'll leave Art alone if his wranglers stay away from our cattle and act civilized in town. Beau's a different matter. If the Pinkertons say he's the man who killed my brother, he gets shipped to Kansas to face murder charges."

Ida wanted to see Beau's back, but hadn't planned on its happening so soon.

"Give me a minute to get changed." She needed her trousers. She couldn't ride Old Molly to a showdown in a housedress. She turned to run back to the farmhouse, but Jared grabbed her upper arm.

"No, you don't," he said. "I don't want you in danger. You take too many chances as it is."

She yanked her arm free. A flush of anger rose up her neck. "This is my fight as much as yours."

"I'm being practical."

"Practical?" she echoed. "I stay here and worry. That's practical?"

He grabbed her shoulders as if to shake sense into her. "The men riding with me have fought wars. They're trained for battle. You have courage, but this'll be different. If Beau refuses to back down, his fight will be to save face. It'll be deadly."

She hadn't lived this many years in Indian country and

lived through the Johnson County range wars without risking her life. She had a pretty good record of coming out on top. "It's not the first time I risked my life. I'm going."

"No, you're not," Jared said. "I'd have a hard time doing what's necessary if I knew you were in harm's way." His voice became pleading. "For once, Ida, do as I ask. Leave this fight to men with military training."

"But—"

He put a finger over her lips. "No buts, Ida. You're a distraction. I can't be worrying about you."

Her heart tightened and her breath came in quick gasps at the thought of Jared in danger without her there to watch his back. Yet, she didn't want to put him in danger. Her insides wrenched as she said what she must.

"Go. Be careful."

* * * *

Ida slumped against the wooden edge of the horse trough until Jared disappeared into the shadows of the night. She gnashed her teeth. No way was she staying put, wondering, worrying. She needed to know for herself that he was safe. She needed to be there when Beau was run out of Johnson County.

Ida paced the packed dirt of the barnyard until an idea formed. If Jared didn't know she was nearby, he wouldn't be distracted.

She chewed on the idea. The more she turned it over in her mind, the better she liked it. She'd ride Old Molly along the creek and onto Campbell property. She'd hide the mare under the creek side cottonwoods and work her way close enough to hear what was going on.

"I hate sitting around, waiting."

Ida turned and ran toward the stoop and into the farm house kitchen. She rushed past Peggy, who was drying the supper dishes, and toward the bedroom stairs. "Why the hurry?" her friend asked.

"I need to get into trousers," Ida answered her over her shoulder. "I'm helping Jared out."

Fortunately, her usually inquisitive friend didn't ask for details. Relieved to get by Peggy so easily, she dashed up the staircase, unbuttoning her housedress as she went. Stripping off the dress, she pulled on work pants that had been airing on a wall hook. She yanked open the dresser and chose a dark-colored shirt to blend with the night-time shadows. Next she pulled on a jacket to protect against the cold which could arrive as soon as the sun was fully down. Satisfied, she started back down the steps. In the kitchen, she collected a pistol from the sideboard and pocketed extra shells.

"Isn't this a romancing occasion?" Peggy asked. "Why the gun?"

"In case I run into a Campbell rider who wants to start trouble."

"Don't you be starting any yourself."

Peggy didn't know the half of it. If her friend knew, she'd have a fit. "I'm taking Old Molly."

"The poor dear has barely had time to rest from all that hauling."

"Can't be helped." Ida was already heading out the kitchen door.

"A beau with that many horses should be able to loan

one to his fiancée, don't you think?" Peggy asked from the doorway.

Courtship was adding miles to the old mare. She'd ridden Molly to the ranch for sherry the other week and once for dinner and once just to talk. "I'll ask."

"You take care of yourself, do you hear? Don't do anything foolish."

When Ida entered the barn to saddle Old Molly, the horse looked resigned to another stretch of work. She positioned the saddle blanket on the mare before hefting the saddle into place. Her heart pounded from the knowledge she was going against Jared's express instructions. She clenched her teeth. She was a woman of action, not a passive female who waited and worried.

After checking that the leather cinch was tight and the bridle was untwisted, she mounted. Tugging on the reins, she guided the tired mare out of the barn and toward Clear Creek.

"Let's go, Old Girl. We'll make sure my man is safe."

Chapter 25

Beau Campbell glared through the dirty front window of his uncle's ranch house at the half dozen prominent Buffalo citizens sitting their horses and waiting patiently for him to answer Jared's shout—among them a banker, the newspaper editor and a store owner. He didn't recognize the man with the handlebar mustache, but his clothes made Beau think he was a shop owner. The others whom he didn't recognize would certainly be equally important.

Tension built around Beau's shoulder blades. He hadn't expected town opposition before he could get his gang fully assembled. He'd thought he'd have more time to build up a following of admirers in Buffalo.

He pasted a smile on his face and gave a friendly wave through the dirt-streaked window. Unhooking the leather straps on his holstered guns to make sure they were ready for action, he maneuvered around the battered settee to open the front door and to stroll leisurely outside. He had his most innocent face pasted on.

"Evening, Gentlemen." He stepped onto the front porch with his thumbs hitched in his back pockets to show he wasn't going for his guns. "What brings you to our neck of the woods?"

"Trouble—and you're the root of it," Jared said.

Beau put on an expression as if he had no idea what the man was talking about. "The foulest of untruths," he said, but with a tone of conciliation to his voice." I don't befoul my den. I'm aiming to settle here."

Jared shook his head, counteracting the denial. "I've been missing cattle since you came to town."

Beau drew up another expression of innocence. "Not a soul in Buffalo has ever seen me driving stolen cattle."

"You're attempting to push Mrs. Osterbach off her land," the store owner said.

"Not push. I made a legitimate offer of purchase for her admirable property. Sadly, she turned me down, but I have high hopes that the lovely lady will reconsider."

"She's not selling," A look of determination settled on Jared's face. "And if she did, she'd sell to me."

That hit Beau like a sledge hammer. He certainly didn't want Jared controlling the water from the farm. He chewed the inside of his left cheek. "Miz Osterbach and I didn't hit it off right away like neighbors should. She holds a grudge against my uncle."

"Don't sully my future wife," Jared growled.

Beau knew damned well that they were betrothed, but he feigned surprise. "Well, isn't that something? Accept my felicitations."

The only response was an uneasy shuffling of Jared's horse. Needing to break the awkward silence coming from the stern-faced men, Beau pretended this was a social occasion. "Why don't you fine gentlemen come along inside?" It was a strain, but he tried his best to sound neighborly. "My dear mother would turn over in her grave if I didn't offer you gents some refreshment."

The men stayed in their saddles. Beau tried again.

"I can't offer you much of the finer things." He poured on the southern charm. "My uncle's home is humble, but I can offer a good grade of whiskey. We'll talk over a sociable drink and straighten out this misfortune." Beau thought he'd sounded imminently reasonable, but the men's faces told him they weren't buying the friendly neighbor act.

"This isn't a social call," Jared said. "We're warning you and your men to lay off Mrs. Osterbach."

"There's been trouble in town, too," the man with the handlebar mustache said.

The condemnation on their faces proved to Beau that he was deeper into troubled waters than he'd first realized. He needed to protest their accusations. "You fine gentlemen have mixed me up with somebody else. I've been meeting right friendly people in town, not causing trouble."

Jared's hand strayed closer to the pistol in his holster. "Don't play the innocent."

Small hairs at the back of Beau's neck stood up even as anger amassed in his belly. He damped down both as he calculated his speed if he had to draw on Jared.

"Cut the lies," the store owner said. "We know you're behind these attacks on the Osterbach farm. Your hired hands were recognized a couple of weeks ago dressed as Indians."

"I saw your men instigate a fight in town," the banker said.

Art Campbell stepped out onto the porch, breaking the heightened tension. He looked around at the men sitting somberly on their horses before spitting tobacco juice off the side of the porch. "What's all this 'ere?"

"These men have complaints against the wranglers, Uncle Art." Beau wanted to divert the attention away from himself.

"I'll speak to them boys," Art said. "They gets liquored up 'n does crazy things."

"One of your men picked my pocket," the unknown man said.

"That I truly regret." Beau figured he knew who the pickpocket was. He'd warned the man to keep his hands to himself. There was too much at stake. "Point him out and I'll send him packing."

Jared drew himself upright in the saddle. His brows were lowered and his eyes glaring. "Let's not pussyfoot around. No more rustling. No more attacks against the farm. No more brawling in town. No more thievery."

Red-hot fury raced through Beau. If it were just the two of them, guns would be blazing. "Harsh words."

"Consider yourself warned," Jared said.

Beau's hands itched to draw both guns.

* * * *

Ida had been forced to get closer to the Campbell ranch house than she'd intended when she first came up with this idea. She was crouching behind a weathered barn door hanging crookedly on its hinges. She'd crept into the barn in time to hear Jared's warning.

While keeping an alert eye on Beau—who stood on the

sagging porch, hands clenched, seeming ready to explode, she caught movement at the bunkhouse doorway and two wranglers came out. Although she saw them, their backs were to her. They were on the side of the bunkhouse away from the line of sight of the townsfolk. One of them was Beau's scary friend. Guns drawn, they sneaked along the rotting bunkhouse wall. The town's representatives sat their horses—unaware, exposed, vulnerable.

Ida furrowed her brow. Protected from the gunmen's line of sight by the shadows cast by the barn door, she could stay quiet or sneak away with Jared none the wiser. But if she did that, would Jared be shot?

The decision was taken out of her hands when the two men stepped from the protection of the bunkhouse with guns aimed at the backs of the men on horseback. Pulling her pistol from her jacket pocket and cocking it, Ida jumped from behind the barn door, shouting, "Drop your guns or I'll shoot."

The men froze. Jared turned to find the source of her voice.

"Nobody shoot," Beau yelled. The Mexican lowered his gun. He motioned to the other man to lower his.

"Miz Osterbach, that you?" Art asked. "Ye' can't hit nothin' from that fur away in this dimness."

"Try me," Ida said and shot at the plumbed tail of the rooster weather vane on the ranch house roof. A metallic ping rang out seconds before the vane spun lopsidedly around its slightly crooked metal pole.

"Guess ya' kin." Art almost seemed to grin.

"What are you doing here?" Anger controlled Jared's voice.

"Helping," she said. "We'll talk later." She hoped her voice sounded calm.

"Ida—" he said, sounding exasperated before she cut him off.

"Finish your business here, and let's go home."

"We said what we came to say." Jared raked his heels along the sides of his mount and guided it toward the opened barn door. The wranglers flattened themselves against the bunkhouse wall, keeping a wide berth from Jared.

Beau rocked back on his heels and audibly released a held breath. His uncle spit tobacco juice off the side of the porch before dropping into one of the porch chairs. The townsmen turned their horses toward the road. The standoff was over.

Ida—feeling guilty that she was caught on Campbell land—lowered her head and stored her gun in her pocket.

"Where's your horse?" Jared's voice cut with an edge.

"Back by the creek."

"I'll take you."

Jared reached down to haul her onto the back of his mount before turning the horse in the direction of the creek. Ida clung to his waist, the tightness in his back muscles against her flushed cheek expressing his anger.

* * * *

Jared gritted his teeth. He wanted to throttle Ida, but contented himself with a question, "What are you doing here?"

"I had to know you were safe."

Her arms were wrapped around his waist. Her cheek

rested against his right shoulder. Her breasts pressed tightly into his back and he could almost count the beats of her heart. Lavender fragrance drifted into the surrounding air. She was alive, but he cringed to think what could've happened if Beau hadn't ordered his men not to shoot.

"You exposed yourself to gunfire." The angst that accompanied his words seemed to sear the air.

"A good thing, too," she murmured into his shirt. "I kept you from getting shot in the back."

He wasn't mollified. "I froze inside when I heard your voice."

"I'd planned to be out of there with no one the wiser," she said. "Those two men changed that plan."

His brows furrowed. "It was dangerous."

"I was protected by the barn door."

"It wasn't enough."

Jared caught the first sounds of the creek. He set the reins in that direction and they came up to where Old Molly was hidden.

Ida slipped off the back of his horse. As she dropped easily to the earth and mounted her mare, he was deprived of her warmth and fragrance. Giving a flick of the reins, she guided Old Molly along the creek and took the lead on the return trip to the farm. The horses picked their way over the darkened, uneven earth. A waning moon cast deep shadows. As they passed by, insects quieted. The closer they got to the farmhouse, the safer he felt for Ida. "You should've listened. I told you to stay at home."

"I'm not that kind of woman, Jared. You'd better understand that now, before we take vows."

They left the creek path and traveled the roadway toward the looming barn. Beams of lantern light beckoned from the farmhouse and bunkhouse.

Jared acknowledged to himself that Ida could and did take care of herself. Although difficult for him to accept at times, it was one of the traits that drew him to her. Isabella's dependency had seemed on occasion to bind him to indentured servitude. Kate differed from her mother in that respect. She was more of a free thinker like Ida. That was probably one of the reasons why Ida and Kate had such a hard time getting along.

"I'll help you unsaddle," he said as they approached the barn's hitching rail.

"I have hired men to help me," she said, shaking her head. "You've had a long day."

He tried one last time to explain himself. "It's not that I want to restrict your freedom, Ida. It's just that I want to keep you from harm."

"You were more exposed than I was." Her tone had an edge to it.

As he rode homeward, his mind was a tumble of unresolved issues. Did he love this woman enough? Ida's stubbornness was why they'd rubbed each other the wrong way over the past years. She'd just warned him that she wasn't about to change.

* * * *

Ida really didn't want to talk about tonight's business until she had more time to analyze the consequences. She turned and slowly walked toward the back steps. She was sure Peggy was waiting for her on the other side of the kitchen door. Her feet dragged, not from tiredness, but from an unwillingness to explain her actions. It wouldn't take long for the news of the altercation to spread about the county. Ida knew she didn't have long to hide the affair from her cousin and Peggy—nor long to hide her quarrel with Jared. She just hoped that she could hide the Campbell ranch news until after she'd had a chance to sleep on it.

Peggy was waiting for her at the kitchen table with two cups of freshly poured coffee. "Where's that man of yours? I'd hoped he'd stop in a while."

"I don't want coffee." Ida pretended a yawn. "I just want sleep."

"Well, if you think it'll keep you awake, I can save it for the morning." Peggy picked up the cup of coffee she'd set out for Ida and poured it back into the coffee pot.

"I'll see you in the morning," Ida said.

"Not so fast," Peggy said. "You never answered me about your beau. Why didn't Jared come in tonight?"

"We quarreled," Ida said by way of the easiest explanation.

"Not again!" Peggy shook her head in disbelief. "You don't even have the date set, do you? Here you two are fussing at each other."

"He wanted me to do one thing and I wanted to do another."

"Just say 'yes' to whatever he asks," Peggy advised her.

"It's not that easy."

"He's a decent man. He'll look to your wellbeing."

"He was asking me to stop thinking and let him think for me."

With a wave of her hand, Peggy belittled the problem. "You're tired. You're seeing things wrong."

Maybe Peggy was right. Maybe in the morning she'd see things differently. Ida's shoulders slumped. Sometimes things were just too tough. She wanted to please Jared, but she didn't want to lose pieces of herself while doing it.

Of the "love, honor and obey" vows, "obey" was always the most difficult for her when married to Dean. Now, she'd had two years of being her own boss. These past years had changed her, made her more independent. Doing as someone else wished would be even harder.

To make a marriage work, she might have to re-learn society's lesson—and obey Jared in all things. Probably Isabella did so to perfection, but could Ida re-learn it?

"I'm going to bed." She headed for the hallway and the bedroom stairs.

"You do that, sweetie," Peggy said, cheerily. "Things'll look better in the morning, won't they?"

* * * *

As he stood on the uneven boards of the ranch house porch later that night, hot anger surged through Beau. It had been a galling confrontation; one that he hadn't been able to control. Art simply sat quietly.

"Those meddlesome bastards wouldn't give me a chance."

Diablo joined them and sat on the front porch step.

"Be glad they gived you a warnin'," Art said. "Them could've laid in wait for us. Could've rounded us all up fer jail."

217

"Those moralizing sons of bitches?" Beau snorted. "They don't have the backbone."

Art rubbed his chin. "Years ago, if faced down, I'da come out fightin'. Then I git smarts. Sometimes it's better not to fight. Sometimes it's better to duck."

The humiliation was too intense for Beau to shrug off. "I want those men eating humble pie."

"¡*Muerto*!" Diablo said. "Get rid of that swine Buell. The rest will fall in line."

"They'll wish they'd never tangled with me."

Art looked at him as if he'd lost his mind. "Then be ready fer a long fight. Them men is serious."

"I'm ready."

"Ya sure that crew of yourn is up fer it?"

Beau scowled. "I pay in gold. They'll fight."

Chapter 26

Two days later, with the sun not yet fully risen to the noon hour in the sky, Ida scrambled out of a furrow and ran toward the edge of the field. She'd been working alone near the fence line to Jared's ranch when she'd recognized his outline against the cloudless sky and waited for him to ride up. He looked frustrated. She embraced his back in a bear hug even as he was dismounting.

He was freshly bathed and dressed like a banker, making the contrast between them all the more apparent. Her clothing smelled of the sweat of her morning labor, but that was trivial compared to an opportunity to make amends. "I'm sorry for making you worry."

He hugged her waist. "You're forgiven."

The apology had been on her mind for two days now. The tenseness he carried in his body had made it imperative for her to apologize—and quickly. She'd just gotten into Peggy's good graces for not telling them straight away about sneaking off to the Campbell ranch. In no uncertain terms, she'd told her to leave that particular fight to the men.

Jared held her close as he spoke. "I'm on my way home

from Buffalo. I saw you working here and decided to detour."

She stepped back to a more proper distance. "I'm glad you did."

"I need to talk with you."

She felt his tension and dreaded what she was about to hear.

"Russ and I went to town early. When we got there we found a telegram for me from the Pinkertons."

Her spine tightened. "Why didn't they send a runner to the Bar J with the telegram?"

"We arrived just as Deputy Trainer was arranging for a runner. Anyhow, the report confirmed that Beau Campbell is my brother's killer. There's an outstanding reward of a hundred dollars posted in Kansas—dead or alive."

Ida tensed. "You're not on your way to shoot it out with him, are you?" He was wearing town clothes, but she had to ask.

Jared spoke with barely controlled anger. "The Justice of the Peace threatened me with jail if I went on my own."

A mixture of pain and anxiety crossed Jared's face. "The deputy is cautious and wants to wait a day. He wants a good-sized posse."

Her heart cried out for Jared. "If it were Deputy Trainer's brother, he'd feel differently."

"The men in Buffalo who came with me the other day want to wait to arrest Beau until after work on Saturday. They don't see the hurry in something a decade old."

"What if he finds out about the telegram? Will he run?"

Jared's mouth set in a grim line. "It's likely he's already

heard. It's hard to keep the telegraph operator from spilling what he knows."

She felt the intensity of his anger. "Beau wanted to become respectable, but that won't happen with him tied to a murder. Everyone will know his history. No doors will open for him. He'll have to leave."

"The only way he can control the town now is by force, but he doesn't have enough men for that." Jared took off his Stetson and wiped an arm across his forehead before resettling the hat. "I may end up chasing after him."

The horse snorted as if anxious to get a move on. Ida swallowed the lump in her throat. If Beau did make a break for it, Jared would go chasing after him—without her. She'd have to live with that somehow.

"I sent Russ to the ranch to organize scouting parties. If Beau makes a break for it, I'll know."

She'd decided to follow Peggy's advice despite her own inclination. That meant she'd stay on the farm while the men rode with the posse. She put a dirt-stained hand over Jared's heart. "I hope he doesn't find out about tomorrow's posse."

"He'd likely set up an ambush to wipe us out," Jared said, "just to show he still can."

Ida shivered and clung to him. "I don't know what I'd do if I lost you."

She hadn't realized, until she'd said it, how true that was. Dean had been relegated to a corner in her heart. That heart would have a gaping hole without Jared.

"You have me here and now," he murmured, nuzzling his nose against hers. His hands caressed her shoulders. "Russ is handling things at the ranch. I won't be needed for at least a half hour. Why don't you take a rest from planting?"

She didn't bother to ask what he meant. She knew. And she was willing.

"I have a blanket in my saddlebag," he added.

"My clothes are all grimy." Ida looked down and brushed at her shirt and trousers in a futile attempt to remove the dirt.

Jared's grin made her flush with pleasure. "I'll just have to get them off you, won't I?"

Some things made her world right again, even when that world seemed to be spinning out of control elsewhere.

Chapter 27

Late Saturday afternoon, Ida pulled the rocking chair out onto the front porch to catch the last of the day's breezes. Trying to keep her mind and fingers busy so she wouldn't worry, she took what pleasure she could in the deepening shadows turning the Big Horn Mountains shades of purple and gray. Jared would be getting ready to ride out to meet the deputy sheriff.

She rocked slowly in the cool of early evening. A large metal pot of potatoes sat on her lap. Thinking she heard the scrape of clothing against wood near the corner of the house, Ida cocked her head to listen.

"Who can that be?" she wondered aloud. She'd been jittery all day.

Peggy was in the kitchen waiting for the potatoes she was supposed to be peeling. The farm hands weren't back from Buffalo yet. Ernest was taking a nap in the bunkhouse.

As she slowly rose from the rocking chair to investigate—the pot of potatoes still in her hands—she caught a glimpse of a man from the corner of her eye. She froze. Malevolent eyes poured loathing above the barrel of a pistol pointed directly at her breast.

"¡*Puta!*"

Instinctively, Ida tossed the potatoes at him and fumbled for the pistol in her pocket. As she screamed for help, she heard a ping like when a copper penny is tossed into a tin bucket at the fair. A tremendous force thumped her chest, shocking her by its severity. Her knees buckled and she stumbled backward to slam against the clapboard wall of the house.

She vaguely heard the metal pot roll off the front porch as intense pain racked her body. As if from a distance, she heard the heavy rocking chair collide with the wooden boards of the porch. A brown fog washed over her, morphing into an all encompassing blackness as she struck the floor.

Chapter 28

Peggy heard the shot, Ida's scream, the metallic roll of the cook pot and the heavy thump on the porch floor. Dropping the towel she was using to dry the dishes, she ran, heart pounding, to the sideboard to grab a loaded pistol. She pushed hard at the dinner bell before she barred the kitchen door. The clanging would wake Ernest, who was napping in the bunkhouse, if he wasn't already awake from the goings on.

She sped towards the front door, her breath coming in short, wheezy bursts. Arriving slightly out of breath, she peered out through the porthole. Curiously, no one was about, not even her friend.

"Ida?"

She opened the top half of the Dutch door so she could see more of the porch and heard Ernest moving around in the bunkhouse. Cautiously, she leaned out the partially opened door. A shape caught her eye. Ida was sprawled on her back on the front porch, blood staining the bodice of her dress. "Oh, my God!"

The blood drained from Peggy's face and her breath

caught in her throat. Ignoring her own safety, she flung open the bottom half of the door and ran to Ida.

"Help!" She sank to her knees beside her wounded friend. "Ernest! Help us!"

She laid her pistol on the wooden floorboards and grabbed a section of Ida's skirt to press it over the warmed blood escaping from just above the left breast.

"Ernest!"

Peggy leaned her weight into the wadded material. The metallic tang of the warm blood assaulted her. Ida was unconscious, her breathing shallow and her skin pallid.

Ernest came rushing around the corner of the farmhouse, pulling up his suspenders. She shouted to him, "Ida's been shot."

His face registered shock. "Will she live?"

"Not if she loses much more blood." Peggy's mind speeded up fourfold. Yet, the happenings around her passed in slow motion. "Get water, clean towels. Bring blankets."

Ernest sprinted into the farmhouse.

Peggy spied the field hands on the road from Buffalo. She released one bloodied hand to wave frantically. "Buck! Hank!" She gestured for them to come to her instead of the bunkhouse. "Over here!"

They spurred their horses and galloped toward her.

Ernest stepped through the doorway with two blankets and a stack of white washcloths and towels. "No shooter in the house." She noticed he'd strapped on a pistol.

Peggy grabbed one of the folded towels as he passed by and tucked it under Ida's shoulder to get the wound off the floor boards. Ernest uprighted the rocking chair which had been knocked on its side. Positioning it within easy reach, he lay the towels and extra blanket on it before carefully tucking a blanket around his cousin. "I put water on to boil. I'll bring a bucket of fresh water while it heats."

"Thank you," Peggy spoke to his disappearing back as he loped toward the kitchen.

The farm hands reined up by the porch steps in a running dismount and tied their horses to the hitching rail. "What happened?"

"Ida's been shot."

"Get the bastard?"

She shook her head. "We've been seeing to her."

Peggy felt strange that—in her worry about Ida—she never thought about whether the gunman was still around. Her pistol still lay on the porch floor. "I was in the kitchen. I didn't see anyone by the time I got outside."

Buck took his rifle from its sheath on his saddle. "We'll look around." He checked the load and slammed it shut before mounting his horse and turning it toward the barn.

"Someone needs to keep pressure on this for me," Peggy said, "while I gather medical supplies."

"I'll do it." Ernest stepped onto the porch, carrying a metal basin and a bucket of fresh water. "I already checked the house, Hank. Scout the out buildings." Ernest knelt and applied pressure to Ida's wound as Hank disappeared on foot around the corner of the farmhouse.

As she rose from her knees, Peggy flinched. Ida's blood had soaked the hem of her skirt. When she held a blood-stained hand out in front of her, it trembled.

Pull yourself together, she chided herself. *You're going to need all your wits about you for this grim business.*

So fortified, she entered the farmhouse to gather up the medicines and bandages.

* * * *

Ernest's heart was bleak. To see Ida like this unnerved him. His once formidable cousin lay helpless—eyes shut, mouth slack, breathing shallow and her head propped awkwardly against the unpainted porch floor. He loved his cousin with a fierceness that burned. His Illinois relatives were far away and he might never see them again. Ida was the foundation of his current family. That foundation lay wounded and unconscious.

Maintaining pressure on the wound, he used the other hand to dip a wash cloth into the basin of cool water. He squeezed out the excess and wiped Ida's pallid face, hoping the dampness would wake her. He was washing blood off her neck when Hank and Buck returned.

"Ain't seen no one," Hank said, "but there's a fresh trail for a single rider headin' south toward the Bar J."

"The shooter ain't from there," Buck said. "Must be a Campbell rider tryin' to put us off the scent."

"I can ride over to the Bar J and warn 'em," Hank said.

Ernest shook his head. "I'll go. They're already on battle alert for the posse, but Jared needs to know Ida's been shot. Best if I bring the news."

"Well, then, what can I do?" Hank asked.

"You need to go for the doctor," Ernest said. "Buck and I need to get Ida off this porch and up to her bed."

Buck dismounted, tied his mount to the hitching rail

and stepped up on the porch. He pointed to the blanket on the rocker. "We can use that to make a stretcher."

Ernest nodded. "That'll work.

As Hank swung into the saddle, Ernest warned him. "More of them might be out there waiting. Be careful."

"I will."

"Tell the doc that Ida's lost a lot of blood. She won't wake up."

"I will."

* * * *

Peggy scurried onto the porch with her basket of unguents and bandages and a pint of whiskey. She'd washed Ida's blood from her hands at the kitchen pump and changed her bloodied skirt for a clean one. As she placed the basket of medical supplies on the wooden flooring beside her friend, she noted that Ernest was maintaining pressure on the wound. "The water's boiling."

"I'll get it," Buck said.

"Fetch it in the china pitcher from Ida's room, if you don't mind. It's easier for me to pour. And clean your hands while you're at it."

Peggy tossed the bloodied water into the front yard, rinsed the basin and set the basin on the porch. "She must've slammed her head when she fell. Otherwise, she shouldn't be out this long, should she?" She wished Ida would wake up and was fretting over her clammy pallor.

"Was she in the rocking chair when she was shot?" Ernest indicated the chair with his head.

Peggy nodded. "She was peeling potatoes. Merciful heaven, it was awful. I heard the pot drop and roll at the same time I heard the shot. She must've been getting up to face the shooter."

"Probably saved her life," Ernest said. "When she moved, the bullet hit near her underarm instead of her heart or lung."

Buck returned with the pitcher of steaming water. He poured some into the basin and used the dipper to add cool water from the bucket. Peggy tested the temperature with her elbow and added more. When satisfied, she poured in some peroxide. She knelt and unscrewed the lids of tin containers of healing ointments.

Relief was visible in Ernest's posture. "One good thing, the bullet must've missed her lung because she's not spitting blood."

"Her breathing's shallow, but there's no hiss to it." When Peggy came close to work on Ida, Ernest released the pressure of his hand and slowly pulled away the soaked wad of skirt. Blood oozed out, but the pressure had staunched the flow.

Peggy bent over her friend and unbuttoned her dress bodice as far as she could without moving Ida's arm. She cut away the material at the shoulder and sleeve with scissors taken from the basket so the cloth could be pushed aside to get at the wound. Wincing at the ugliness of the bullet hole, she steadied herself emotionally to pull out fibers embedded in the torn skin. After cleansing the oozing wound with peroxide water, she dribbled whiskey over it and applied healing herbs. She took a white-cotton bandage, folded it and asked Ernest to hold the pad in place.

Ernest walked to the edge of the porch and poured water from the dipper over his hands to rinse them. He returned and held the pad in place.

"I need to see if the bullet is still in there." Peggy spoke as calmly as she could muster, considering that her friend was hovering near death. Anxious as she was to get Ida to a bed, she knew she must work meticulously or she might overlook problems. "If you please, Buck, we need to roll her onto her side."

The field hand squatted on the same side as Ernest and they gently rolled Ida toward themselves. "It's a good thing she landed on her back," Ernest said. "The porch floor staunched the flow."

As Buck steadied Ida, Peggy pulled away the bloodied material to find a jagged exit wound. "Thank the Lord. The bullet came out!" She wouldn't have to probe for the bullet or anxiously wait out the hours for the doctor to arrive. Pus and fever would be less of a risk.

Working as fast as was prudent, she cleaned the jagged skin, applied ointments and powders to encourage healing, and asked Ernest to hold another pad of white cotton over the wound. She searched through the medicine basket for her widest and longest bandage to wrap around and hold the pads in place.

"The bastard, pardon my French, must've been sure of himself," Ernest said. "He didn't stick around to make sure she was dead."

"From the time it took me to get to the front door from the kitchen, he could've finished her off." Peggy shivered at the thought.

"The pot saved her, too," Buck told them as he indicated the pot with a jerk of his head. "Look at that there crease."

"It deflected the bullet," Ernest said.

"Count our blessings." Peggy wrapped the bandage over the pads and several times around Ida's chest and shoulder. She tucked the end of the bandage under the wrapping and checked that no blood had trickled out before securing Ida's left arm with a sling to immobilize it.

Relief flooded through her. This part of Ida's care was ended, but she braced herself. She needed to nurse her friend entirely out of danger.

* * * *

Ernest held the top corners of the blanket while Buck held the bottoms. Together, they maneuvered the improvised stretcher around the sharp-angled corner of the stair landing and through the narrow doorway into Ida's bedroom. Peggy had gone upstairs ahead of him with her basket of medicines and bandages to open the shutters to fresh air and fold down blankets.

"How do you want us to do this?" Ernest was relieved they'd gotten his cousin up the narrow stairway without mishap. "I think we should move her as little as possible."

"Put her down on the bed, blanket and all," Peggy said. "It can protect the mattress."

He and Buck carefully placed the Ida-laden blanket on the bed.

"We'll need to roll her onto her good side." Peggy bustled around the bed, straightening it. "We'll need pillows to prop her up."

"I'll get them," Buck said.

"Get the extra two in my bedroom and the bolster," she said. "Just leave the one for me."

Ernest, his heart heavy, helped Peggy unlace and remove Ida's shoes.

When Buck returned, he and Peggy rolled Ida onto her side while Ernest tucked the bolster behind his cousin. Then he tucked the pillows tightly in front to prevent Ida from rolling onto her injured shoulder. When satisfied, he pulled up the blanket.

"I wish she'd wake up," he heard himself saying.

"Nothing we can do about that," Peggy said as she busied herself around the bedside, "but we can make her more comfortable. Bring a couple glasses of water and a tablespoon. I need to get some water into her to make up for all that blood she lost."

Buck turned toward the door. "I'll get them." He was already heading down the stairs.

"And bring a pitcher of hot water, if you will." Peggy straightened the blanket on the foot of the bed. "I need to soak some white willow bark to dull the pain."

Ernest braced his shoulders. Although he hated to leave, he must. All that could be done medically was being done by Peggy. Hank was on his way for the doctor. Buck could keep an eye on the place against further attacks. "I'll ride over to the Bar J to let Jared know what happened."

He turned and clattered down the stairs before anyone could object.

* * * *

When Buck came back with the water and a tablespoon, Peggy sent him downstairs to get the pot of honey and the vinegar on the kitchen sideboard and a jar of dried blackberries. She tilted Ida's head to spoon water between her parched lips. When he returned, she mixed some honey, vinegar and blackberries into the second glass of water and fed the concoction slowly to her friend to ward off fever. She asked Buck to check Ida's head for any bumps that would tell them why she was still unconscious.

He poked his fingers into the braided hair, pausing on the left side. "She's got a goose-sized lump under here. No bleedin' tho'."

"When I get a chance, I'll unbraid her hair. She'll be more comfortable that way."

"Are you going to get her out of those bloody clothes?" Buck asked.

"The bleeding's stopped. I don't want to start it up again by moving her."

"Anything more I should do before I go out to scout around the place?"

Peggy looked up at the field hand.

"Throw a bucket of water over Ida's blood on the front porch, will you? I don't want Jared to see it when he comes."

Chapter 29

Jared looked up from digging mud out of his stallion's hooves and cocked his head to listen. Someone was riding hell-for-leather toward the ranch. Working inside the stable like he was, he couldn't see who. He let the stallion's leg drop and pulled out his pistol. Stepping out of the doorway, he saw his soon-to-be cousin by marriage on the road and put the gun away. Unease lined Ernest's face. He was tying the reins to the hitching post at the water trough when Jared came up to him. The winded horse was one of two geldings he'd loaned to the farm. "What's the matter?"

"Ida's been shot. It's pretty bad."

A sledge hammer hit Jared in the stomach. "When?"

"About an hour ago. Luckily, the bullet went straight through. Peggy patched her up and Hank's going for the doctor, but she's lost a lot of blood and hasn't come around yet."

"I'll go to her." Jared turned toward the barn and his horse.

"Wait," Ernest yelled.

He halted.

"The shooter's trail led in this direction.

Acid pumped into Jared's stomach.

"I followed the trail from the farm, but lost track of it before I got near the ranch house," Ernest said. "We think the shooter was Beau Campbell and that he's coming for you." He removed his wide-brimmed hat and wiped the back of his hand across his brow before resetting the hat.

Jared scowled, looking grim. "I'll put Russ on the alert. I have to get to Ida."

He'd waited years to avenge his brother, but he'd have to hand the settling of that score to his foreman. Ida's well-being was more important. "I wasn't home when Isabella sickened. I was chasing after that bastard. She died without me at her side. I won't fail Ida."

A look of sympathy crossed Ernest's face. "She's not awake. There's nothing you can do right now. Peggy and Buck are looking out for her."

"She needs me." His voice sounded strangled.

"What she needs now is to know she'll never again be threatened by Campbell's gang."

"It's hard not being there."

"For me, too," Ernest said. "She must've heard something. She was getting up from the front porch rocker when it happened and because she was moving the bullet missed her heart."

"I can't lose her." Jared's world was crumbling.

"All that can be done is being done."

"I need to see for myself."

"Then I'll ride back with you. It's not safe for you out there alone."

Jared nodded. This he could accept. "I need time to ready my horse and leave instructions with the men."

"Sure." Ernest turned toward the ranch house. "I'll go up to the kitchen for coffee."

"Ask Rosalie to pack supplies for Russ and a dozen wranglers," Jared said. "The posse may need to ride for days. Beau's good at hiding."

Jared instructed a stable boy lingering within earshot to find Russ and to round up the men—especially those most recently hired who were handiest with a gun.

"Tell them it's urgent. My fiancée's been shot."

* * * *

After cleaning the last two hooves in the sunlight at the stable door, Jared led the stallion toward the tack room deeper in the darkened stable. He'd just lifted a saddle off its wooden peg when he heard the faint click of a boot heel against the packed earth floor. His breath caught. Someone was sneaking up on him.

He turned and heaved the saddle in the direction of the sound. From the corner of his eye, he saw Beau Campbell leap out of the way and drop behind the wooden barrier of a horse stall. Jared slapped his horse on its rump, sending the stallion racing out the opened barn door. He dove to safety behind the wooden wall of the nearby stall and he drew his pistol. Breathing hard, he eased his body toward the stall opening so he could cover any attempt to rush him. "How many did you bring with you, coward?"

"I don't need help for an old fart like you." Beau laughed, mockingly. "I've been listening to you miserable cretins talk. Nice of you to send that farmer and boy away so we can face each other man-to-man. You hounded me for years. Today, it's your turn to bite the bullet."

"You swine. You'll never get away."

"Oh, it'll be mightily tough for me to escape, but I've had a multitude of practice."

"I'll kill you."

"Try it."

There was no target for Jared to shoot at. He cocked his ears, trying to pinpoint where Beau crouched. He didn't want his men to blunder in and get shot for their troubles.

"I was unhappily surprised," Beau said from his hiding place in the horse stall, "that your fiancée isn't dead as a door nail. It's unlike Diablo to miss his mark. With luck, she'll pass on to the pearly gates."

So Diablo had pulled the trigger!

Anger so furious it almost blinded him roiled to life. Jared threw caution to the wind. Gun drawn, he stood upright and shot at the horse stall where Beau was hiding. Time slowed as the bullet smacked uselessly into wood. He was reorienting himself and turning to the right when Beau rose and fired. The bullet whizzed past Jared's ear.

He shook off fear and moved back into firing position. Instead of ducking for cover, he pulled the trigger rapidly twice, gratified to hear a startled grunt.

Beau's body slowly toppled forward over the wooden barrier and sprawled face down onto the packed dirt of the barn's floor. His new Stetson hat spun off his head to land in trampled straw and muck. He lay, unmoving, knees bent, his lower legs held vertical by the wall of the horse stall. His arms were flung out as if a supplicant in a church.

Jared studied his dying enemy as a dark pool of blood formed near Campbell's chest. For almost a decade, his mind's eye carried the slaughter of his sister-in-law and brother. That bitter image faded as the light left Beau's eyes. Finally—the score was settled.

Chapter 30

The smell of the gunpowder clung in the air and assailed Jared's nostrils. Heightened awareness, a residue of battle, slowly receded, even as the resonance of gunfire in enclosed quarters still reverberated in his ears. He heard a commotion outside and turned toward the sounds. Ernest and the others rushed into the Bar J stables. Jared holstered his weapon. "It's over."

"What happened?" Russ looked around as he holstered his own gun.

"Campbell was lying in wait. His shot missed. Mine didn't."

Ernest walked over to Beau and lifted him by the blond hair. Looking relieved that there were no signs of life, he allowed the head to drop onto the dirt floor. "Ida will be safe now."

"Not yet. Beau said Diablo was the one who shot Ida. He's still out there." Despite Jared's own need to be at Ida's side, he recognized the need to break up the Campbell gang to make her truly safe. He must make sacrifices in the moment to settle this strife once and for all. "Art Campbell and the rest of Beau's gang must understand that Ida is to be left alone."

Jared turned to the wranglers. "Someone find this murderer's horse. We need to take the body to his uncle."

A stable boy and a wrangler ran toward the back door to search outside. Several men went in the opposite direction.

Jared glanced out the barn door at the angle of the sun. "If we're going to travel, we'd better get started. Deputy Trainer should be arriving at the Campbell ranch just about now."

He retrieved his saddle from among the bales of hay where it had landed. Placing it over a stall rail, he whistled for his horse before speaking to his foreman. "Russ, pick three men to ride to the farm to protect my fiancée."

"I'll ride along with them," Ernest said. "I need to be with my cousin."

"I'll come as soon as I can." Jared caught the bridle of his horse as it halted in front of him. "Five of you stand guard here. The rest ride with me to the Campbell ranch."

Russ picked which men should stay and which should go to the farm. Ernest followed the men who headed for the corral and their horses.

Jared retrieved his tack and threw a saddle blanket over his horse. He hoisted the leather saddle into place, tightened the cinch and led the horse outside to wait for his men to saddle up.

The stable lad and wrangler arrived, leading the reins of Beau's horse with the body draped over the saddle and tied on. Eventually, all the wranglers returned with saddled horses. Jared assigned a wrangler to trail Beau Campbell's horse.

Jared yelled, "Mount up."

The Bar J horses kicked up considerable dust as the men rode rapidly north across the meadow to return Beau Campbell to his uncle and put an end to the fighting. The outlaw had lost all ability to instill fear—or exact revenge.

Chapter 31

Peggy ushered the portly doctor into the darkened farm-house hallway. She was struck by how his jolly manner seemed at odds with the life and death circumstances he was called upon to resolve.

"I'm glad you're here," she said to Doctor Phillips. "Dear Ida hasn't regained consciousness yet."

"Lead the way, Ma'am. I'll take a look at her."

Lifting her skirts with one hand, Peggy lit his way up the narrow stairs with an oil lamp. Upon entering the bed-room, she placed the lamp on the mahogany bedside table. She crossed the room to a lamp dimly glowing on the oak washstand and turned up its wick. Even with a considerably brighter room, there was no reaction from Ida. Peggy returned bedside to fuss with the covers. "I'm relieved you can stay the night, Doctor Phillips. We made up a bed for you in the bunkhouse."

"Too late in the day to travel anyway," he said.

"I feel better with you here. I don't like the look of her."

"Now, now," the doctor said, soothingly as he approached the bed. "I've dealt with plenty of gunshot wounds. I'll patch her up."

"That's what I'm counting on, aren't I?"

"Your two farm hands said they'd unhitch my wagon and feed my horse," the doctor said as he stood by the bedside watching Ida breathe.

"That they will," she said. "You can depend on them."

He placed his black-leather medical bag on the floor, shrugged out of his pinstriped, black frock coat and red-paisley vest and handed them both to Peggy. She left to hang them on the clothes rack in her bedroom. If she got a chance, she'd brush them before he left tomorrow morning on his return journey to Buffalo.

The doctor had rolled up his shirt sleeves when Peggy returned to Ida's bedroom. She pointed to the washstand with its basin of warmed water and bar of lye soap. "I like to keep a sick room clean." She handed a towel to the doctor for drying his hands.

"And I'd like to get the smell of horse off my hands." The doctor took his time washing up, running the washrag over his face and hair and underneath his loosened collar. When done, he re-buttoned the collar, but left his shirt sleeves rolled up. He turned toward his patient. "Now, let's take a look at what we've got here."

Peggy pulled down the covers and untied the sling keeping Ida's injury immobile.

The doctor looked satisfied that no bleeding started as he was removing the bandage. "Do you know who did this?"

"We think it was the neighbor's nephew, Beau Campbell, but Ida never woke up to tell us for sure."

"I'd heard they were having some kind of trouble."

Peggy chewed her lower lip. "He wants this farm and its water."

The fears of the past months came rushing in. She shook away her anxieties and told the doctor, "Ida won't sell out. Especially to a Campbell."

"She thinks Art deliberately killed her husband, doesn't she?" the doctor asked.

"I believe it, too."

The doctor got Peggy's help to lift their patient so he could look under the bandage on Ida's back. "This is going to scar."

Peggy winced. She'd guessed as much.

He probed the shoulder and chest with gentle pressure. "At least it went straight through and didn't hit bone. It could've caused a lot more trouble. What have you done so far?"

Peggy explained what had happened since she found Ida bleeding on the front porch. "I also bandaged on some Sioux healing herbs. I've used them last year when Buck's arm got torn open by fencing wire. Those gashes healed fast. I'll show the herbs to you."

She crossed the room to her basket of medical supplies and brought back a leather pouch containing dried herbs. The doctor probed and sniffed and looked satisfied.

"To keep Ida's fever down, I used wild flower honey, blackberry and vinegar in a glass of water. And white willow bark." She lifted the bedside lantern to give more light as the doctor bent over Ida.

"No sign of pus." The doctor used a metal instrument to

pull aside the torn flesh and look inside. "You did a good job. It doesn't need to be cauterized."

Peggy couldn't help but feel pleased. She'd done her best and her best might just save her friend's life.

"I'm going to stitch this up as neatly as I can. No use scarring her any more than necessary." The doctor searched in his bag and brought out a thin strand of cat gut and a long needle. "With such healthy skin in there, I don't anticipate a fever, but just in case, I'll leave some of this sulfur powder behind when I go tomorrow. And some opium for the pain."

Just then Peggy heard a commotion in the barnyard. Her heart dropped to her stomach. "Oh, Lord, don't let them be Campbell men."

She put the lantern close by the doctor on the night stand and ran to the window. She opened it enough to lean out to watch the riders converge on the farm. One of the voices belonged to Ernest. Peggy pulled her head back inside. "Do you think you can handle the stitching up without me, Doctor Phillips?"

"As long as Ida doesn't move. If she wakes up, I'll call out the window."

"Some Bar J men are here with Ernest," Peggy explained. "The shooter was going in their direction. I want to find out the news."

* * * *

Peggy scurried down the bedroom stairs, crossed the kitchen and looked out the kitchen door. It had gotten darker while she was upstairs with the doctor. She went back inside for the oil lamp before crossing the packed dirt towards the barn.

Polite Enemies

The wranglers were leading winded horses to the water trough. Buck stepped out of the bunkhouse with a shotgun in hand. Hank came out of the barn, having gotten the doctor's carriage and horse stowed for the night.

"What happened?" she asked as she rushed up.

"The boss shot and kilt Beau Campbell," a wrangler said as he dismounted.

"The fool tried to waylay him in the barn," another rider said. "The boss sent us here to stand guard, jest in case any other Campbell man wants a go at you."

"Thank goodness that man can't hurt my Ida any more," Peggy said.

"He bragged Diablo shot 'er," the wrangler said as he tied his horse to the hitching rail at the water trough.

"Oh, dear," Peggy said.

"How is Ida?" Ernest asked.

"She's holding her own. The doc's stitching her up now."

"Has she come around yet?" Hank asked.

Peggy shook her head. "No, but the doctor doesn't seem worried. He says her body's trying to heal itself by keeping her asleep." She looked around. "Where's Mr. Buell?"

"He took the body to Art Campbell. He'll make sure that gang can't harm Ida any more and come after it's all over."

Peggy harrumphed. "Well, they better not be too long about it."

Ernest removed his wide-brimmed hat and ran his fingers through his hair. "I'll go up to sit with her," he said, putting the hat back on and starting toward the farmhouse. "You can have a break."

247

"Me, too," Buck said.

Peggy raised a hand to stop them. "Only after you wash up. I keep a clean sick room."

Although they grumbled, they promised to wash up and put on clean clothes.

"I'll put supper on," Peggy said. "None of us has eaten this dreadful night. I bet the doctor will be hungry."

"Sounds good to me."

"Only left-overs, I'm afraid," she said.

"As long as it's filling," Hank said.

"You'd better keep this." Peggy handed the lantern to a Bar J wrangler. "I can find my way without it." She started for the kitchen, but stopped and turned back. "Someone needs to do the night feeding of the animals."

"I'll do it." Buck rested his shotgun against the bunk-house.

"And I'll show the men where to bed down," Hank said.

"The doctor's bunk is already made up," Peggy said from the back steps. "You'll have to toss a coin for the rest of the empty beds."

"Anybody left over," Hank said, "is on the first shift of guard duty."

As she made her way through the dark barnyard toward the light from the open kitchen door, Peggy heard Hank say to the Bar J men, "There's plenty of feed in the barn for your horses and room on the tack pegs for your saddles. Make yourselves comfortable. We'll set up guard duty rotation when you're settled in."

Chapter 32

Jared and the Bar J wranglers rode as hard and as fast toward the Campbell ranch as the descending darkness allowed. While still about a mile away, they met up with the posse on the road from Buffalo, which was delivering the warrant of arrest for the murder of Jared's brother and sister-in-law. The cloud of dust kicked up by their horse's hooves settled around the men from town.

"I was expecting only you, Mr. Buell." Deputy Trainer looked puzzled. "Why are there so many of you?"

"Campbell tried to ambush me in our stables." Jared waved forward the wrangler towing Beau's horse with the body.

"But the boss," the Bar J wrangler said, "he drew faster. Plastered 'im between the eyes, he did."

The deputy looked relieved.

Jared spotted the sheriff in the posse—a burly bull of a man, who looked like he could take on any three men at one time. He was just the kind of man to take the burden of shutting down Beau's gang off Jared's shoulders. "Angus, when did you get back in town?"

"Last night."

Jared brought the posse up-to-date on the shootings at both the farm and the ranch to the sounds of a few "damns" and "the bastard."

"Changes things, don't it?" The sheriff rubbed his chin. "Can't serve a warrant on a dead man."

"There still might be a dustup," Jared said. "Campbell's men might not take kindly to his death when they realize their leader won't be paying their wages."

"It's best if the whole gang leaves," the storekeeper said. "My wife's afraid to walk Main Street for all the hooligans loitering there."

Another of the men from town spoke. "They may scatter and run when they hear about Beau."

"Maybe, maybe not," Jared said. "What if someone's been waiting for a chance to take over?"

"Maybe Art's got control," the deputy said.

"Old Rattlesnake ain't got no sting these days," a Bar J rider said.

"Art's old and sick," Russ said, "but that doesn't say the rest of them are."

"I'll arrest any one of them gets out of line," the sheriff said. "Trainer, you'll stay back here with a few men to make sure nobody gets away. Spread out. Don't stay bunched up."

He turned to the remaining men. "The rest of you town men stay spread out, but ride with Mr. Buell and me. We'll ride up to the front door and see if we can't talk some sense into Art."

Jared hoped this would be the case. He wanted this resolved so he could get to Ida.

"You Bar J men," the sheriff said, "divide up and arrive at the ranch house from various angles."

"It's getting dark," a Bar J wrangler grumbled. "I like to see where I'm shootin'."

"We oughta git moving," another man said.

The new moon was only a silvery sliver in the darkening sky. It would be of little or no help when the blackness of night finally settled in.

"No shooting unless it looks like they're ready to shoot first. Let's ride." The sheriff spurred his horse toward the Campbell ranch with Jared trailing Beau's horse slightly behind him. The rest of the men scattered into assigned groups.

For a while, only hoof beats intruded on the stillness of the evening. Then the rustling sounds of night scavenging animals moving through the brush seeped into Jared's consciousness. Life continued, no matter what tragedy was going on.

* * * *

As Jared trotted his stallion towards the dilapidated Campbell ranch house, trailing Beau's horse, he was on the alert for any hint of danger. The men announced themselves when they got near the house. A couple of kerosene lanterns had been brought out onto the sagging porch to provide light. They could see Art, but it must have been difficult for him to make them out in the dusk. He sat on a porch bench, chewing a cud of tobacco. "Is that me nephew slung over that horse?"

"It is."

"Told 'im he was biting off more than he could chew."

A bottle of whiskey sat by Art's right hand. He raised it to his lips and swallowed before saying, "I needed that. Keeps the pain down."

"Mr. Campbell," Sheriff Angus said, "your nephew started the fight with Mr. Buell."

"Tried to warn 'im, didn't I? Wouldn't listen. That's what he gits." Art spat juice at a spittoon near the bench, missed and it splattered the porch.

"I have a Kansas warrant for his arrest for bank robbery and murder," the sheriff said. "I'll contact the court to let them know he's deceased."

"Me nephew thought he'd got clean away with that littl' matter." Art rubbed his chin. "Told 'im he was foolin' hisself."

They were silent a while as Art Campbell chewed his tobacco cud. The chirping of tree toads by the creek melded with distant shouts as they waited. Jared broke the silence. He needed a quick resolution to this matter, whether with words or guns. "My fiancée's never again to be worried about raids."

"We don't want no trouble in town either," the sheriff said.

"Too old fer trouble," Art said. "You planning to jail me?"

"I'm considering it."

"Too crippled up fer jail. Besides, I'm inheritin' Beau's bank accounts. Moving meself back east to where the doctoring's better."

"Some of that money is stolen," Jared said. "The law will have to sort out the bank accounts."

"There'll be enough left over. Plannin' on sellin' the ranch, too."

Jared would willingly buy Art's ranch just to get the man out of sight. While Art was here, he was a constant reminder to Ida of her murdered husband. Jared would tear down the dilapidated buildings and leave the land fallow long enough to get the grass entrenched before moving cattle on it each winter. "I'll make you a fair offer if you agree to leave town."

Art grunted. "Ye got a deal."

"Where are Beau's riders?" the sheriff asked.

"Skedaddled. The scout saw ye lawmen comin' with me nephew tied to hiz horse. Them didn't stick around to have a chat, like I'm doin'."

"Diablo Avilos with them?" Jared asked.

"Headin' for Mexico by his lonesome."

"Some of the boys will go after him," Sheriff Angus said. "They'll track him down."

Jared handed the reins for Beau's horse to one of the townsmen.

"Thank ee, Mr. Buell, fer bringin' me nephew home."

"Do you want us to put him in the parlor for you?" Sheriff Angus asked.

"No siree," Art said. "He's too much fer me to move and I ain't sure my own wranglers'll stick 'round after t'night's goings on."

"What shall we do with him?"

"Take 'im into town. Tell the undertaker I'll come by wagon tomorra to buy 'im a box."

A couple of townsmen agreed to take Beau's body back

to Buffalo. They left, trailing the horse, as Russ and the Bar J men arrived from either side of the ranch house. "Seems quiet enough."

"Angus will tell you all about it," Jared said. "You and the boys should help out. He'll need to make sure all of Beau's gang left town. I need to get to Ida."

"Get outta here," the sheriff said. "We'll handle things."

Beau and his gang had stolen enough of his energy and time. Ida was his focus from now on. Let the posse track Diablo. This time he was staying by the side of the woman he loved. Almost five hours had passed since he'd learned Ida lay wounded—hours during which she may have slipped away from him forever.

"I'm done here." He kicked his horse into action.

Chapter 33

The rigid control Jared had forced on himself since learning Ida had been shot was rapidly slipping. He brushed his horse's ribs with boot heels, urging the stallion into a gallop.

Bypassing the road, he cut across earth recently rutted by flooding. A moonless night shadowed the meadow landscape, distorting its features. Sadness as black as the night sky enveloped his heart. As he hurtled recklessly across uneven pasture, his frayed spirits swung between hope and fear.

If Ida was still unconscious when he arrived at the farm, he'd sit at her bedside until she awoke. If need be, he'd drag her back into the land of the living by the sheer force of his will.

Only now did he realize how much he'd sacrifice to keep her in his life. Whatever it took, he would do—even if it meant moving out of the ranch house and onto the farm. She'd brought a passion into his life that he wouldn't live without, even if it meant estrangement from his daughter.

Chapter 34

Jared saw the lights from the farmhouse even before he left the meadow to ride along the farm road. He galloped the remaining yards to the barnyard. As he pulled up, Hank stepped out of the kitchen door.

"How's Mrs. Osterbach," Jared asked.

"The doc's pleased." Hank crossed the barnyard. "The wound was a clean one. No pus."

"Is she awake?"

"Not yet, but the doctor ain't so worried. He's in there eatin', if you want to ask 'im."

"I'll go upstairs first."

"Best use the front door then," Hank advised him. "You come in the kitchen and you'll be waylaid. They awantin' to hear what happened at the Campbell's."

"That can wait," Jared said. "I need to get to my fiancée."

"Well, then, let me cool your horse for you," Hank said. "It looks like you rode him hard."

"That'll be a help." He dismounted and handed the reins to the farm hand.

Jared crossed the barnyard at a trot, climbed the front steps and stepped over the threshold of the partially opened door. He was about to climb the bedroom stairs when Peggy came into the hallway from the kitchen. She shook a metal soup ladle at him.

"Where do you think you're going, mister?"

At the iron command in her voice, Jared stood stock still and doffed his hat. "To see my fiancée."

"Not like that, you're not."

Anger mingled with frustration. His heart sank. *Now what?*

"I'm not having you track dirt into a sick room now, am I?" Peggy pointed the ladle at his riding pants and boots. He looked down. His clothes and boots were caked with road dust.

Peggy placed her hands on her hips, the metal ladle angled to one side. "All that dirt could make dear Ida take a turn for the worse." She shooed him back down the hallway and out the front door as if he were an intrusive chicken. "Get along now. Wash up proper like."

"Yes, Ma'am," was all he could say.

"And get the boys to give you some of Ernest's clean clothes. You two are about the same height."

Delay was maddening, but he'd heard of sick people developing fevers after visits. He couldn't chance setting back Ida's recovery by being obstinate.

"And clean those dirty boots of yours," Peggy added for good measure.

One of Jared's wranglers yelled from the kitchen. "I'll ride to the Bar J, boss. I'll get your own clothes."

257

Jared heard the scraping of a chair as the wrangler rose to go. "While you're there, ask Mrs. Sanchez to bring the wagon early tomorrow with some cooked food."

"Will do, boss."

"Tell her to get ready to stay here for a few days," Jared said. "Mrs. Knapp has enough to do without cooking and cleaning for us, too."

"That's a kindness," Peggy said. "Rosalie will be good company."

Hank appeared at the front door with a lantern. "I have to wash up and change clothes," Jared told him.

"Follow me," Hank said. "I'll git you set up for a wash in the bunkhouse. Mrs. Knapp is very strict about them things."

Peggy and her ladle and were heading back toward the kitchen. She added over her shoulder, "I'll have a plate of hot food ready when you come back."

Jared stepped out of the door and started down the porch steps as Ernest came around the corner of the farmhouse.

"Shouldn't you be with my cousin?" Ernest asked.

Hank answered for Jared. "I'm takin' him to the bunkhouse to wash up. Mrs. Knapp insists."

"I'll show Mr. Buell what to do."

"There's a full milk can of fresh water in the bunkhouse," Hank said. "Take this here lantern so you ken see what you're doin'."

"You see Ida yet?" Ernest asked as they walked across the packed earth toward the bunkhouse.

Jared shook his head. "Got caught before I put one foot on the stairs."

Ernest laughed. "Peggy's good-hearted, but she runs a strict household."

"She offered me some of your clothes, until mine get here." Jared suspected he'd swim in them because Ernest was a much broader man.

"I'll pick some out."

Jared meekly followed as Ernest lighted the way across the barnyard. This wasn't his ranch, not his territory. Here he obeyed orders, he didn't give them.

* * * *

Even in the dim lantern light, Ernest could see the anguished twinges pass across Jared's face. The man wanted desperately to be with Ida. Ernest speeded up his step. He'd help Jared get to the sickroom as quickly as possible. "It's good you're here. She'll need you when she wakes up." Ernest knew his cousin's heart.

"I want to marry her," Jared told him, "as soon as she wakes up."

"You'll be good for her. She's carried too many burdens these last two years."

Jared grimaced. "She'll be stubborn about giving them up."

Ernest chuckled. "Don't I know! I've tried."

In the bunkhouse, Jared stripped and washed with lye soap and tepid water. Ernest opened the worn dresser drawer and selected a set of clothes and some socks. He walked back to where Jared was drying off.

"These pants might be a little wide."

"They'll do until I get my own."

"I have suspenders you can use," Ernest said. "There's a clean pair of long-johns."

"I'll make do."

Ernest had thought the rancher might be demanding and hard to please. After all, Jared built and ran the largest ranch in the county. He probably had more money than any two business owners living in Buffalo. But his cousin's future husband was accepting without complaint whatever was handed to him. Ernest already felt a brotherly kinship with the man.

"I'll get someone to brush these boots for you." Ernest picked up the dusty boots and headed out the bunkhouse door. When he arrived at the barn, Hank had just finished putting up Jared's horse for the night. The Bar J wranglers who would stay overnight had gone to the kitchen for supper. Their horses seemed to be settling in. Ernest explained to Hank what he wanted done.

When he returned to the bunkhouse, Jared had almost finished dressing. "Let's go in by way of the kitchen. You need some food in you."

The rancher shook his head. "Hank said to steer clear of the kitchen. The men will pounce on me for news. I'm surprised they haven't mobbed me already."

"I suspect Mrs. Knapp's keeping them in line." He could see Peggy threatening the men with her soup ladle if they interfered with anything that would upset her friend.

"I'll go right upstairs."

The rancher had just finished buttoning the shirt when Hank dropped off the boots. Jared pulled the newly brushed boots on over the pair of clean cotton socks and declared himself ready as he as stumped the boots on.

"You should eat something first." Ernest said. "You

won't do Ida any good if you break down your own health."

Frustration crossed Jared's face. "I'm tired of these holdups."

"At least take a platter of food up with you."

"That, I will do."

As they crossed the barnyard to the front door, a Bar J rider rode up to tell Jared that Beau's gang had totally cleared out. Only Art and his wranglers remained. The sheriff was heading back to Buffalo to telegraph the Kansas court and to make arrangements for Art's trip back east. The sheriff and the posse would arrive at the farm at dawn to pick up Diablo's trail.

"Get some food in the kitchen," Jared said, "and stay long enough to let them know what happened tonight. Keep everybody off my back."

Chapter 35

Jared's heart wrenched violently when he reached the sickroom. Ida's breathing was shallow and her eyes sunken. The robust woman he'd fallen in love with was gone from that weakened frame.

A lump rose in his throat. Jared placed his platter of food on the bedside table's lace doily and walked toward the bed. The doctor was draping a damp compress over his fiancée's pale forehead. "Let me do that."

"Gladly," Doctor Phillips said. "I need another break. My food's getting cold." He rose from the bedside chair to let Jared sit.

"You sure she's doing all right?" Jared had patched up men wounded in battle, but this was his Ida. She was an essential part of his wellbeing. A vise squeezed his heart, just looking at her helplessness.

"Her pulse is a little weak," Doctor Phillips said, "but steady. The shock's wearing off. You'll need to watch her carefully."

"I will." Jared smoothed the damp cloth over her forehead. When he touched the skin, it was clammy.

"She'll start to come around and could be in a lot of pain," the doctor said. "You'll need to watch out for that."

The lump moved higher in Jared's throat. The women of his household took care of the sick. He'd never needed to learn the refined ins and outs of the personal care the sick required. He gritted his teeth and took in a deep breath. He'd sacrifice sleep—learn nursing skills—anything. "What do I do?"

Doctor Phillips showed him how to sponge Ida's face and neck with a wet washrag. "The dampness will soothe her," the doctor said as he wrung out another cloth. After removing the earlier one, he draped the wet cloth over the lump on Ida's head and arranged it across her temples. "These cloths dry out from her body heat. You have to keep replacing them."

Jared nodded to show he understood.

The doctor demonstrated how to tilt back Ida's head and spoon water between her lips. "We have to keep her from dehydrating. Do this pretty often. She needs to replace that blood she lost."

"I can do that."

"Be careful she doesn't choke. Only let it dribble in."

Doctor Phillips explained about the medicine against fever. "No more than two teaspoons at a time," he warned. "And make sure she swallows. If she can't swallow, tilt her head way back and rub her throat until she gets it down." The doctor demonstrated. He showed where the bed pan was and extra towels and washcloths. "Don't touch her bandage."

"Why not?" Jared was curious to see the wound, to

know for himself the damage done by Diablo Avilos.

"I don't want her stitches to open."

Jared reined in his curiosity.

"Anything else before I go downstairs?" the doctor asked.

"If she's in pain, what do I do?"

"Let me know immediately. I'll take care of the pain with a dose of laudanum."

The doctor wiped his brow with his shirt sleeve and looked Jared in the eye. "If you don't feel at ease in a sick room, I'll stay or get Mrs. Knapp back up here. Otherwise, I'm heading downstairs to finish my supper."

"I'll be all right."

"That's about it then." The doctor turned toward the bedroom door. "Call me if she wakes up."

"I'll call," Jared promised.

Doctor Phillips disappeared through the doorway and Jared heard his shoes clump down the stairs. Ida's wellbeing now lay fully on his shoulders.

Chapter 36

Jared bent to kiss Ida's cool forehead before laying a fresh, moist washcloth across her brow. "My love, return to me."

He sponged Ida's face and neck. He dribbled honeyed water between her parched lips. His hands felt too big for the tasks, but with determination he fulfilled each small step. The full measure of his love flowed into this pale woman lying so still.

Taking a fresh washrag from the washstand drawer, he sponged her hands. He pushed back her sleeves to wash her forearms lying above the covers. Awkwardly, he bent over the bed to straighten the covers. He was all thumbs, but determined. He lifted Ida's head slightly so that he could fluff up the pillow. He was hopeful of her recovery. She no longer had a fever and the wound hadn't festered. He knew she couldn't hear him, but it was important to say aloud what was on his heart.

"I'd send for the pastor right now if I knew you'd say 'I do' when you wake up."

She lay there, unresponsive. His heart missed a beat.

"My love, I decided I can live on the farm. My daughter and mother-in-law can take over the ranch house. I don't care."

Jared willingly made this promise.

"I'll have my mother's diamond resized for your engagement ring. I'll buy the most expensive wedding ring in Sheridan." He wove tales of their life together. Outlining their future while she slept. Her helplessness clarified for him the insignificance of the obstacles that earlier had seemed insurmountable.

Peggy poked her head through the opened doorway on her way to bed. She asked if he needed anything before she went to sleep. Seeing her reminded him of the neglected food. He reached out to pick up a chicken leg.

"Take your rest," he told her. "I'll shout the house down and wake everybody for miles around if she takes a turn for the worse."

After Peggy closed her bedroom door, Jared ate the now-cold food and returned the empty plate to the night stand. He changed Ida's compress and sponged her pallid skin, making sure the blankets were tucked in and the sling securely in place. Feeling the exhaustion of the day, he decided to rest his eyes. His stomach also needed quiet time to digest the meal. He lowered the lantern's wick. Taking Ida's hand into his—so he could be instantly alert if she stirred— he let his head fall back against the high-backed chair and slowly closed his eyes.

Just for a minute, he told himself. *I'll rest my eyes for a moment.*

Chapter 37

Ida's eyelids fluttered briefly then opened slightly. The bedroom was grayed with shadows. The sounds of a rooster told her dawn was approaching. Her head throbbed. Her lips felt parched. She was disoriented. Her lashes created a screen through which she studied her world.

The quiet bedroom was dimly lit by a kerosene lantern. The washcloth lying on her forehead had dried as if hours had passed since it was changed. She was terribly weak and her shoulder ached abominably. With reluctance, she remembered the man who'd shot her. That's why she ached.

She cringed when the sounds of male voices and horses being saddled drifted in from the barn. She relaxed when she realized there was no urgency to the sounds. No outlaws could be nearby. She wondered how long she'd been unconscious. *At least from supper time to near dawn,* she thought.

Someone's hand rested on hers. Ida turned her pounding head slightly on the pillow so that she could see whose hand it was. Jared dozed by the bedside, his chin propped on his chest. He looked haggard and drawn.

A warm glow spread throughout her. She had much to

say to her lover. She was ready to commit. No more barriers thrown up.

Ida watched him breathe and occasionally murmur in his sleep. When she felt strong enough, she called out to him, "Jared."

Her voice sounded hoarse and feeble to her ears. Startled, he lifted his head and stared.

"You're awake." He sounded groggy and disoriented. He rubbed his eyes. "I must've fallen asleep." He leaned over to remove the dried washcloth and placed the back of his hand on her forehead. "No fever."

Jared bent to kiss her forehead. His lips were cool and he smelled of lye soap. She noticed he was wearing Ernest's clothes.

"Are you in pain?"

"A little," she lied. She wouldn't confess the degree of her pain until she'd let him know the conviction that arrived full blown when she'd awakened.

"I'll get the doctor," he said. "He's sleeping in the bunkhouse."

"Not yet." Her voice was weak, but it was enough to stay his rise from the bedside chair. "I need to talk with you."

"At least let me re-dampen this cloth." He dipped the washcloth in a basin of water, wrung it out and placed it on her forehead. She relished its refreshing moistness. He put a spoonful of honeyed water to her dried lips. "I was so worried about you. I'm so sorry I fell asleep. I was exhausted."

"No harm done." She needed to let him know what happened. She needed to share that terrible time. "Diablo Avilos shot me."

He squeezed her hand, reassuringly. "I know. Beau's dead. I shot him. The posse will track Diablo from here this morning. He's heading for Mexico."

Relief flooded through her. "And you're all right?" She couldn't move enough to see if he was wounded.

Jared nodded. "He ambushed me, but his shot missed. Mine didn't."

She lay quietly, conserving her strength, wishing the throbbing in her shoulder would go away and wishing that Jared still held her hand. "How long have I been out?"

"Just overnight," he said.

"Not too long."

"Doctor Phillips said your body was healing itself as you slept."

"It has a ways to go." She managed a grin.

She should be getting to the heart of what she needed to say. Instead, she found herself nibbling around the edges as she found out what had happened while she slept. "I've been listening to men saddling up."

"Those are my wranglers. They're joining the posse."

"Where's my cousin?"

"With the posse," Jared said. "He told me last night he feels it's his duty. I'll make sure he comes to see you before he leaves."

"And Peggy?"

"She's in her bedroom. I haven't heard her stirring. She was exhausted last night."

"Poor thing."

"Peggy found you yesterday and nursed you until the doctor took over."

"She's a blessing." Ida asked for more water and got down several soothing spoonfuls as Jared explained the events at the Campbell ranch. "Art is selling his ranch to me."

"Thank God—no more water disputes."

"The rest of Beau's gang left the county when they learned their paymaster was dead. You'll be safe now."

She could get on with her life—just as soon as this dreadful pain went away.

Jared raised her dry hand to his lips. "You lost a lot of blood. Peggy probably saved you from bleeding to death."

Ida drew his hand toward her face and leaned her cheek onto it. "I must talk with you."

Jared looked serious, like he was afraid of rejection. "I love you, Ida. I want to marry right now—no waiting."

Her heart beat faster. They were the very words she had for him.

"I'll live on the farm. Anything to be near you." The strength of his commitment vibrated in the air.

"I won't ask that of you," she said. "You're a rancher through and through. You'd be miserable on a farm."

"I'll manage. His kiss pinned her head into the pillow and put pressure on the pulsating bump on her skull. She didn't care. The joy traveling through her was its own narcotic.

She hated bringing problems into the light of day, but in all practicality, they needed to be said. "What about your daughter? She won't approve."

"My daughter has no say in this."

"I'm no good at social functions. I'm a farmer."

"It's the determined farmer in you that I love." He nestled her hand against his unshaven cheek. "You aren't a substitute for Isabella and I don't want to be a substitute for Dean."

"You're loved for yourself, Jared." She turned her head to kiss his hand before saying, "Dean will always have a spot in my heart, but you lay claim to all the rest."

He caressed her hand with his thumb. His love had a rejuvenating effect on every inch of her. Even the throb in her shoulder made no difference. "I'll move to the ranch. Somehow, I'll survive your daughter and mother-in-law."

He chuckled over her bluntness. "They'll have their own section of the ranch house. We'll have ours."

"That's good."

"They're in Sheridan and showing no signs of wanting to come back anytime soon. They may not even come for our wedding."

"That will give me time to settle in." Ernest and the hands would have to do the farm work alone much of this year. She'd be busy planning a wedding and a honeymoon. "We'll marry as soon as I'm strong enough to stand up and take my vows. I want a wedding in the grove of aspen by the creek. I want to invite all our friends."

"That's settled then." Jared pulled away and stood up, shaking out his shoulders as if they were stiff from the way he'd slept. "I'll wake Peggy and get the doctor to check you over."

"Wait."

Ida hated spoiling this beautiful moment, but there was one more barrier.

"I'm willing to live on the ranch as much as I can, but there'll be days of planting and harvest or some emergency when I'll need to stay here at the farm."

"I already thought about that and have a solution."

"What?"

"I don't care how you fill your days or at which household table we eat. I don't care whether we sleep at the ranch or at the farm. The only thing I care about is that we end up at night in the same bed."

Ida could happily live with that condition.

ABOUT THE AUTHOR

JoAnn is a graduate of the University of California, Berkeley with a double major in English and Social Science. She has her Masters in Teaching in English with an E.S.L. minor from Fairleigh Dickinson University and her M.B.A. studies from Pepperdine University.

Her debut medieval romantic suspense novels, *MATILDA'S SONG* and *OUT OF THE DARK*, received four stars from *RT Book Reviews*. JoAnn's agent—Dawn Dowdle of Blue Ridge Literary Agency—recently sold EXPECT NO TROUBLE, a paranormal suspense novel which will be released April 2014.

She likes to walk, swim and read. She lives in Northern California.

To learn more, please visit www.joannsmithainsworth.com. Send an email to jsa@joannsmithainsworth.com.

*For your reading pleasure,
we invite you to visit our
web bookstore*

WHISKEY CREEK PRESS

www.whiskeycreekpress.com